DEBILITATED RELATIONSHIPS

by

Dominique Webster

Debilitated Relationships

Acknowledgement: To my family for the love and support and a special dedication to my grandmother because she inspired me to follow my dreams.

Intro

WHO SAYS DYSFUNCTION CAN'T WORK?

As a child, you never know where your life will go. This is not your typical everyday family. For starters you have, Prosperous, who is religious and very successful. Antenatal, is the pregnant one that can't seem to look at a man without getting pregnant. Dynamo, married for the wrong reason, but manages to stay true to the vows he made. Princess of Darkness who was created as Dynamo took her upon his wing; Liberty, who is the most educated one but has the hardest of time being loved and depends on her books to get her through any hardships; Malady, who has a lifelong disease but yet lives as if she will live forever but has Mettle as her recent companion and finally; Rhizome the root of this family that seems to be the glue to bind things together. Each member has their own journey and how they have lived that journey and overcome those obstacles will be revealed.

Chapter 1

Liberty sat in the sterile lobby waiting patiently for her mother to emerge from the double doors. The scent of disinfectant and floor wax caused the contents of her stomach to swirl, but she was determined to tough it out. Truth of the matter was she had no choice but to tough it out. Her mother expected—demanded—that of her.

The clock on the wall read three forty-seven. Thirty minutes of waiting had taken its toll. Liberty tossed the magazine she'd been pretending to read on the coffee table, thought about what she was going to say when she barged into the examination room, and then sprang to her feet.

From behind a counter, which was enclosed in plexi-glass, the condescending receptionist with the nasally voice, bad wig, and a bad attitude, must have noticed Liberty's agitation. Even from that distance she could see Liberty nostrils flare and the way she stared at the doors that led to the examination area.

"Umm, ma'am," said the dictator who sat on the other side of the plexi-glass. Her annoying voice came through the holes in the plexi-glass that were designed to allow the disrespectful orders she barked make it to their targets, "you can't go back that there."

There is an old saying: *sometimes it's better to ask for forgiveness than to get permission.* Liberty was about to show anyone watching just how that saying looked in real time.

Her frustration was apropos. She went to the car to grab some paperwork. When she returned to the lobby, her mother, Malady, had already been taken into the examination room to hear the results of the most important medical exam of her life. Liberty slid the paperwork through the slot to the receptionist and prepared to be buzzed in, but the condescending heffa wouldn't press the button to unlock the door.

Liberty stated her case, the bully stated some bullshit company policy. They stared at each other—Liberty lost. The receptionist was drunk with power and knew how to use it.

After sitting in that lobby watching a group of conservatives on Fox TV make excuses for the Commander-and-Chief, Liberty's patience ran out. She had every intention to dart through that door the next time a patient walked out and there was nothing anyone—especially the witch behind the plexi-glass was going to do to stop her.

The doorknob twitched. The door slowly opened. Liberty prepared to make a dash. The receptionist pointed and shouted something Liberty ignored. And then…her mother came out.

"Malady! Are you okay?"

"Where were you?" Malady asked. Her voice was shaky; lathered in stress.

"I was stuck out here because she," Liberty pointed at the frowning receptionist, "wouldn't open the door and let me in." As they walked in front of the window Liberty unleashed. "But that's okay, because after the letter I write, and will be addressed to every doctor here, explaining how you treated me and my mother, you'll be lucky to still have a job."

Malady patted Liberty's hand. "Don't worry about it child. She got the devil in her and ain't worth the effort. People like that are just rotten to the core. If there weren't folks like that, we wouldn't be able to spot the good people. It's natures balance, baby. Just get me to the car."

Liberty held her arm out so that Malady could grab it. They strolled side-by-side to the car. It was a slow walk because Malady couldn't move fast. Liberty didn't mind. If it had taken an hour to get from the entrance of the doctor's office to the car, she would have been by her mother's side without any sign of impatience.

Once they were seated inside the car, Liberty turned the key to get the engine growling and the air condition going. The weather outside was at ninety degrees and climbing, sitting in an idling car with no air condition would have landed them both in that doctor's office as patients.

7

"Well, mama, would were the results?"

Malady pointed her crooked finger at the front window, "Let's just go, baby."

"Malady...I didn't sit in that lobby for nearly forty minutes waiting for you to come out so that you can act like you don't have something worth telling me. What did the doctor say?"

Malady sighed. Pools of water formed in her eyes. She lifted her shaking hand and gave Liberty the paper that she squeezed until it was completely wrinkled in the middle.

Liberty studied the paper. "Malady," she whispered, "this says that—"

"The tumors have spread to my lungs and in my lymph nodes. I have less than six months to live."

The only thing shaking harder than Liberty's hands at that moment were her own lips. A tear streaked down her cheek. She closed her eyes and leaned forward until her forehead rested on the steering wheel.

"Now, now, child...this ain't no surprise. We both know my cancer has been getting worse."

"But, mama—"

"But nothing!" Malady said. "You been coming with me to these appointments since we first learned I was sick a year ago. You and I both know the situation was getting worse." She reached over and rubbed Liberty's shoulder. "There is a reason why out of all my children, I wanted you to be the one to come with during this process—because you're the smartest and the strongest. I knew you would know you would give me the best advice on how to proceed, and most importantly, I knew you could keep it a secret until I was ready to tell the family."

"We've got to tell'em, mama. They deserve to know this."

"I know." Maladay removed her hand from Liberty's shoulder and then wiped the tears that were streaming down her own face. "I want you to do something for me."

Liberty nodded. "You know I'll do anything for you, mama."

"I know you would, baby," Malady flashed that smile that routinely stopped traffic and lit up rooms her entire life whenever she flashed it. "I want you to round up everyone so we can have one last family dinner at Thanksgiving."

"That's less than a month away."

"I know it's going to be hard because they act like they can't stand to be around each other for more than ten minutes, but I want you to get'em together. I'll break the news to everybody at the same time."

"What about daddy? When you gon' tell him. It ain't right to break this kind of news to him in front of everybody."

"I know child," Malady said and waved dismissively. "Don't you worry about your daddy. I've been dealing with Rhizome for forty years. I know when and how to say stuff to him. You just round up your siblings."

"I'll figure something out, mama."

Malady smiled and pulled Liberty over for a hug. While the two embraced she whispered into her child's ear. "I know you will, baby. You always do."

Chapter 2

Dynamo walked around the motor pool inspecting the vehicles and reveling in the worried looks on the young soldiers faces. He was known for being a hard ass. The only sergeant who seemed to enjoy in making the soldiers under him work beyond normal duty hours.

"Private Johnson, did you decide to bypass the wheels on this truck?"

"No sergeant!" the pimple faced young man replied.

"Well, explain to me why all of this mud is still caked on the rims."

"I...I must have overlooked it, sergeant. I'll clean it up."

"You damn right you will. And you gon' stay here all night doing it if that's what it takes." Dynamo looked at the other three soldiers watching him give Private Johnson a hard time. "You know what, since y'all didn't make sure he did it right, the three of you can stay here after hours and help him reclean this vehicle."

They all unleashed a collective moan.

Dynamo was about to give them all a verbal tongue lashing, but stopped when his cellphone buzzed in his pocket. He glanced at the screen and scrunched his face when he saw Liberty's name.

"Liberty what's up?"

"Hey Dynamo, did I catch you at a bad time?"

Dynamo looked at the soldiers hustling to help scrub the wheels of the 2.5-ton truck.

"No, I'm good. What's up. I haven't heard from you in a while."

"It's mom."

"What about her?" Dynamo asked.

"She wants us all to get together for Thanksgiving."

"Damn sis, I wasn't planning on coming home this Thanksgiving."

"I know. I heard. But mom really wants us all to come to dinner. She insisted I call you because she really wants you to be there."

Dynamo sighed. Eating turkey and dressing at the house of his many female companions during Thanksgiving was his plan. Besides that, getting from Ft. Stewart, Georgia to Dallas, Texas was no easy task. It was easily a thirty-hour roundtrip drive that he wasn't sure his car could make. Because Thanksgiving was only three days away, the cost of a plane ticket would be astronomical. The desire to decline was eating away at him, but there was something about Liberty's tone that let him know he shouldn't.

"Alright," Dynamo said. "I'll talk to my First Sergeant in the morning and request a few days of leave. I'm going to have to try to get a plane ticket—that might not be easy because this is last minute."

Dynamo stayed away from the family because of his poor relationship with Rhizome. Things between the two of them had been bad since Dynamo decided to join the military instead of takeover the lawncare company Rhizome when he was a young man.

Liberty could hear how her brother was trying to find an excuse to back out of the request, but she wouldn't let him.

"Great! I'll let mama know you're coming. This is going to make her day."

"Yeah, it might make her day, but daddy will probably grunt and roll his eyes."

"Stop! We're not having that drama between y'all two this year. This is an important holiday for mama, and you and daddy are going to have to find a way to squash y'all tension…at least for this Thanksgiving. If y'all wanna go back to not speaking to each other after that, then that's on y'all."

"I hear you," Dynamo mumbled.

"Good. See you in a few days. Love you."

11

"Un-huh," Dynamo grunted. He hung up, more annoyed than he was before she called. Since taking his frustration out on Liberty wasn't an option, he looked at the struggling soldiers and took it out on them. "Y'all still doing a terrible job. Just rewash the whole damn truck!"

Chapter 3

Being the middle child is hard. Antenatal wasn't the middle child per se, but she was the third and the second of three girls, so trying to be noticed and heard was a challenge for her.

Malady seemed to instinctively know that life for Antenatal would be challenging, so they did all they could to make things easier for her. Their first attempt at making the chocolate beauty feel special was giving her an Afrocentric name that would be something everyone would be sure to talk about for years to come.

Ironically, none of the efforts they made to make her feel special seemed to work. Antenatal was a handful from the moment she learned to walk. As she grew older, her propensity for doing the things her parent warned her not to do became greater.

Antenatal's rebellious ways led to her becoming the first of Rhizome and Malady's kids to make them grandparents. Her hard-headed ways landed her in the unenviable position of being a single parent.

Liberty tried to help her younger sister whenever she could, but that proved to be hard because Antenatal was always resistant. No matter how badly she needed help, the idea of accepting assistance from Liberty, the more successful and childless older sister, proved to be too hard of a pill to swallow.

While sitting on her couch in an apartment that wasn't much bigger than the bedroom at her parent's house, Antenatal watched her favorite television show and downed cashews.

"Hello," Antenatal said, wasting cashews on the front of her shirt and the sofa.

"Natal, this is Liberty. Are you busy? I need to talk to you."

"If I told you I was too busy to talk would you let me go?"

"No. I need to talk now."

"Then I guess I'm free to talk. What's up?"

"Thanksgiving is what's up. Are you still coming to mama's house?"

"Yeah, I'm gon' pass through and get something to eat because you know I'm not cooking."

"I need you to do more than just pass through. Mama wants to have a family dinner. I need you to come at a certain time and be prepared to stay a while."

"No. You know I don't do all of that. I ain't trying to sit around the table and listen to everybody take turns telling me what I should be doing with my life."

"Natal, stop exaggerating. No one is going to pick on you."

"Yes, y'all will. That's how it always ends up. Don't make me remind you of what happened last Christmas."

The previous Christmas was a disaster. All the kids decided to swap gifts at their parent's house. At the last minute, Dynamo suggested they make a game of it by playing White Elephant.

Antenatal didn't want to play, but knew that refusal would make her look like the lone malcontent. She agreed, and thirty minutes later, found herself holding a Christmas snow globe instead of the Kindle eBook Reader that was given to her. Per the rules of the game, she had to give up her gift. What seemed like a harmless game to the others resembled more of a metaphor for life to Antenatal. Being stuck with the scraps instead of life's biggest prizes was all she knew.

"Natal, I've said this to you before, and I'm going to say it again—not everything is about you. I'm gon' need you to get out of your feelings and do this for mama."

An awkward silence kept them tethered to the line. Eventually, Antenatal sighed and spoke up.

"Alright, but I'm tellin' you now. The moment I feel y'all are tryin' to use me as a punching bag, I'm leavin'."

14

Liberty knew there was no sense in arguing with her stubborn sister. She'd gotten the commitment she was looking for, so it was best to leave it at that.

"Good. I'll let mama know you're coming."

Chapter 4

Prosperous was the youngest of Rhizome and Malady's children. She was the child that everyone adored. Born with creamy skin that looked like coffee after the cream has been dropped in it, she was the beneficiary of the type of favor that the world has heaped on light-skinned blacks. That same favor also seemed to come her way from her parents—a fact that angered her siblings.

Out of all the Watership kids, Prosperous seemed to be the one with the least amount of restrictions. A lot of that could attributed to the fact that she was the youngest. By the time she was entering high school, Rhizome and Malady had grown tired of parenting. Not because they didn't love their kids, but because they were just flat out exhausted.

Besides, Prosperous was so ambitious and focused that she made their parenting job easier. When she was in elementary school she went to Malady and told her which high school she wanted to attend.

"Who chooses a high school before they are even finish with junior high school? Where do these people get this make a choice here and make a choice there?" Malady asked.

Prosperous looked at her mother and said, "I've done the research mama, and I know which school will give me the best chance in life."

"You may think you know what's best, but you're too young. You're going to go to school that is designated for this area."

Liberty and Antenatal were both very athletic so they were bused to schools outside of the district because of their athletic skills. Prosperous wasn't athletic at all, but she was very smart.

"I am so over people telling me what I have to do even though I know what's best for me," she pouted.

"Sorry baby, but that's just the way it is," Malady said. "Someday you'll be old enough to make your own decisions."

"What if I decide that I want to go to Antenatal school my freshman and sophomore year and transfer to Liberty's school my junior and senior year; will they allow me to do that?"

Malady looked at her spunky child and smiled. Even then she knew that nothing or no one would stop Prosperous for accomplishing things. At that moment, she knew that they'd given her the perfect name.

Malady loved her kids all the same, but it took a few weeks before Rhizome could warm up to Prosperous. The fact that he, and the rest of his kids, was dark-skinned and Prosperous wasn't made him have doubts about paternity in the beginning. Those doubts melted away like an ice cube on the hot pavement once he spent time with the beautiful newborn with the big round eyes and thick eyebrows that seem to meet in the center of her head.

Liberty tried several times to track down Prosperous to tell her about the family Thanksgiving dinner, but failed. Prosperous became very religious after high school and was into saving souls. She was on a religious retreat when Liberty reached out and took a day or so to return the call."

"Hey Liberty," Prosperous said, "I saw you called a few times."

"Yeah, I've been trying to reach you. Where have you been?"

"I was in California for a few days working with some people about my church's on-line ministry. Is everything okay?"

Liberty thought long and hard about telling Prosperous about their mother's condition, but decided not to. She'd avoided spilling the beans to her other siblings and figured it wouldn't be right to only tell Prosperous.

"Everything is fine. Mama asked me to round everyone up. She feels it's been too long since we all were together as a family and she wants to have a big Thanksgiving celebration."

"Ooh, that sounds good. I can use a break. I'll definitely be there. Do I need to bring a meal?"

"No, just bring yourself—and a guess if you have one."

Liberty took every chance available to pry into her younger sister's love life, but always hit a brick wall. Prosperous was extremely private; never introducing any of her boyfriends to the family.

"Stop it," Prosperous replied playfully. "You need to worry about your own date."

"I don't have one, but I know you do."

"Maybe I do, maybe I don't."

"Well, whoever he is, bring him to the dinner."

"I'll think about it," Prosperous said. "What about Dynamo and Natal, are they coming?"

"Dynamo tried to back out of it, but I wouldn't let him. Natal was just being herself—"

"Let me guess…crying about everyone picking on her."

"You know it. I promised her I wouldn't let that happen. She's coming."

"Good. I miss y'all. Let mama know I'll be there. I've gotta run. See you soon. Love ya!"

"Love you too, sis."

Chapter 5

Malady sat in her high-back chair working on a crossword puzzle and sipping coffee. Doing those two things, at the same time, were the ways she passed the time. Her children were all grown. Rhizome was rarely home because he was always out overseeing the crews that he hired to do the landscaping jobs. Her only grandchild, Diamond, rarely came around because Antenatal always had an attitude. So, the puzzles and her coffee were the things she did to keep herself busy and not focus on the fact that she was dying of cancer.

When she heard her husband's, truck pull into the driveway it startled her. Rhizome never came home before nightfall.

"I'm home!"

Malady glanced at the hands on the grandfather clock in the corner of the living room. "You're early today."

"I know. The boys are on top of it today. Everybody showed up for work, so all of the jobs got done on time for a change."

Rhizome went into the kitchen and grabbed a beer from the refrigerator. He came back into the living room and sat down in his recliner.

"The remote is right there," Malady said and pointed at the coffee table.

"Thanks. I'm gon' try to catch the game."

While Rhizome surfed through the channels in search of the baseball game, Malady stared at him. Their love affair went back decades. Thoughts of their life together flashed across her mind.

Malady was getting ready to enter her senior in high school when she met the most handsome boy she'd ever seen. He was tall and drop dead gorgeous. His caramel complexion and chiseled face made him look intense. His physique was so impressive that she thought he could have been on a college football or basketball team.

When she asked her friends who he was, they all laughed and said his name is Rhizome. Her girlfriends immediately went into matchmaker mode. Everyday they'd ask her if she would date him if he approached. Malady's response was consistent, "Only if he is in high school."

What Malady didn't realize was that Rhizome would be the man to change her life. The first guy that she would ever date would also be the only father to all her children.

It was a hot summer evening and since Malady was one of the basketball team stars, she had to make sure that all her grades were up to par so she could remain eligible to play. She decided to do something that she had never done before—go to summer school to get ahead of her studies.

The first day of summer school, she entered class with the assumption that it would be a breeze. However, Malady had no idea that Rhizome's mother—a strict disciplinarian and a stickler for studying—would be her Summer School teacher.

As Malady, sat in class, the guy that she had once asked her friends about showed up at the door. Malady didn't know that Rhizome was the freshmen quarterback and that he and his family were already well known around campus.

One day, when class was getting ready to be dismissed, she got up and accidently bumped into Rhizome. Sparks and whistles seemed to go off and fire seemed to sizzle up in her bones. She knew that she needed to get away from him, but was frozen in her spot. The energy and passion she felt from Rhizome when he touched her made her know that he would change her life forever.

As time went by, Malady knew that the attraction she felt for Rhizome was dangerous. She tried to stay as far away from him as she could. Each day, she would see him in the cafeteria and avoid looking his way. If she saw him coming toward her in the hallway she would often turn and walk in the opposite direction. For an entire month, she followed this process, and it seemed to work…for a while.

On the last day of summer school, Rhizome approached Malady,

"What's your name?" Rhizome asked.

Malady flashed a smile that showed all thirty-two of her teeth, which proved she was flattered, but her response was the perfect one to give to a boy who was accustomed to girls flocking around him. "I don't just give my name out to strangers. If you want to know who I am, ask around."

The response was as unexpected to Rhizome as the hook on a fishing line is to a fish when it bites into what appears to be a floating worm. When she walked off after giving him this response, he couldn't help but smile.

The first day of her senior year, all her friends seemed to be focused on scoping out the cute boys, but all Malady was focused on was basketball. Malady was the youngest of eighteen children and her parents were merely less fortunate people. She knew that she wanted to do as much as she could this year to get a scholarship for college because her family couldn't afford to send her to college.

As Malady entered campus that first day of school, she saw that handsome guy whom she encountered at summer school.

"That's him!"

"Who?" all her friends replied in unison.

"Rhizome. I told y'all that I saw him in summer school, but when he asked my name, I told him to go ask around to find out. Do y'all think he asked around?"

Her girlfriends laughed and looked at her as if the joke was on her. "Malady, he's the captain of the football team he just transferred to this school. Everyone knows him."

"I don't. Why was he at summer school? Is he dumb or something?"

"No. He's supposed to be real smart. His mother is a professor over on the college campus, but she also teaches summer school for the high school."

"That explains why I saw him at summer school every day. He walked around like some type of big shot."

"Rhizome," Malady said and placed her puzzle on her lap, "have I ever told you when I first fell in love with you?"

Rhizome's eyebrows arched when he heard the question. He placed the remote on the coffee table, leaned back in his chair and looked at his beautiful wife.

"You told me once. I believe you said it was when you first saw me at summer school that year my mother was your teacher."

Malady smiled and nodded.

"Where did that question come from?"

Malady shrugged. "I don't know. I was just thinking about it. You are still just as handsome today as you were back then."

Rhizome blushed. He leaned over and touched his wife's knee affectionately. They weren't big kissers at this point in their lives. A loving touch was all they needed to make each other feel special.

Rhizome smiled and leaned back in his seat. He looked up at the ceiling and reminisced.

"Did I tell you about how I searched for you when school started back up?"

"You told me," Malady said and smirked, "but I feel like hearing it again."

Rhizome smiled and continued to talk while staring up at the ceiling. He was as wide-eyed as he was the first time he went to a drive-in movie theatre. The ceiling was the huge screens and the memories of their younger days was the film being shown.

"Me and my friends were standing against a wall watching all the new faces. That's when I spotted you. You were talking to your girlfriends, and dribbling a basketball."

"I was such a tomboy."

"Yes, you were." Rhizome smiled. "When I saw you, I asked them your name." He looked over at Malady and wagged his finger. "You told me if I wanted to know your name I needed to ask around."

"I sure did."

"That's right. So that's just what I did. My friend Bezzie said, 'Dude, you might as well keep scoping out these other chics. She is a senior; you ain't got a shot hooking up with her.' A second boy chimed in. 'I heard she's gay. Nobody has ever seen her with a boy.' I ain't pay no attention to those fools.

"Bezzie was the biggest fool of them all," Malady said. "I never liked him."

"Yeah, old Bezzie was hard to like, but he was a good guy. I didn't believe it when he said your name was, Malady."

"Why?"

"Because it sounded like something out of a Shakespeare story."

Malady giggled.

"Anyway, I made my way to class feeling better that I'd learned the name of the cute girl I'd met that summer, but then I lost you."

"You didn't lose me because I never left. You stopped looking for me."

"That's not true, honey. I used to look for you every day, but could never find you. After three weeks, I got tired of trying to find you myself and finally told me friends. I started asking them if they'd seen you. Come to find out, that fool Bezzie knew where you were the entire time."

"He was dumb as a bag of rocks," Malady said and picked back up her crossword puzzle.

Rhizome grinned. "Yeah, he could be at times. That boy looked at me and said, 'Man, how is it that you play football and have no clue about what really goes on, on campus? Bezzie asked. "Malady is the star of the basketball team. I could have been told you where to find her, but I didn't know you were that interested. She is at practice right now. If you want to see her then hang out after practice and you will see her as she leaves campus.'"

"The best advice he ever gave you."

"Yes, it was. I waited at the back door of the gym where everyone used to leave out. When you came out that door, I damn near peed in my shorts. You were so doggone cute."

Now Malady was blushing. "What was that corny line you shouted?"

"When I saw you come out, I yelled, 'Malady is what I hear they call you!' You spun around and started smiling." Rhizome pointed at his wife. "Yep, that's the smile right there."

Malady waved dismissively. "Stop trying to make me blush."

"It's the truth," Rhizome said.

"I was impressed. I knew you had gone through some effort to find out my name. However, I was curious as to know why you were so hell bent on wanting to know who I was."

"Do you remember what you said when you came over?"

"Yep," Malady said. "I walked over to you and asked, 'How do you know my name? Who told you?' You looked at me and said, "No one ever really tells who their source is. Just know that when I want something, I don't give up on it.'"

"Ahhh, that was smooth wasn't it?" Rhizome asked while grinning from ear to ear.

"Almost as smooth as me telling you to find out who I was."

They both took a moment to laugh. Now Malady was also staring up at the ceiling watching the same movie of their past.

"It must've been another three weeks after that day before I saw you again," Malady said. "All I wondered about during those weeks was whether you liked me or not. I wondered what it was about me that you so attractive. All of those silly questions ran around in my head."

"You were thinkin' 'bout me, huh?"

"I wanted to see you again so badly. At lunch I used to look for you."

"You know we had different lunch periods."

"I know, but that didn't stop me from hoping I'd see you, but I never did. Then it happened one day. You appeared, but with a girl on your arm. I was heartbroken. I started to lose self-confidence because for the first time I was interested in a guy who appeared to be interested in me, but turns out you was

24

interested in other people too. I started to wonder if I'd made a mistake by playing hard to get."

"I wouldn't say that," Rhizome chimed in. "I was young and dumb. When I didn't see you, I thought you'd moved on. I was popular, so I was just enjoying all the attention that came my way. Besides, I didn't know you were looking for me. When I finally ran into you again, you gave me the cold shoulder."

"I sure did," Malady said. "As far as I was concerned, you chose that person over me."

Rhizome laughed. "After you dissed me, I ran across the yard to try and catch up with you. I wanted to know why you gave him such a rude stare. I had no idea that the girl you saw me with was your cousin."

"Yes, my cousin, Muliebrous."

"But we were just friends."

"I know that now, but I had no way of knowing that back then. The fact that she only liked girl didn't come out until we were older."

"When I asked you why you were giving me the cold stare and didn't say hello, you said, 'You have all the "hellos" and "how are doings" right across the yard.' When I realized you were talking about Muliebrous all I could do was laugh. You tried to walk away and I grabbed your arm." Suddenly, Rhizome's wide grin vanished. "That was the day I found out Draco liked you."

"You thought you were the only one with admirers," Malady said and chuckled.

"I thought wrong. That fool approached me in the hallway. He thought that since he was the Captain of the football team, he could intimidate me. I asked what class you were in and ole boy tried to call me a bitch."

"Draco had been flirting with me for years. He had always had a thing for me, but I never paid him any attention. When his friends told him, I liked you—I guess they found out from my friends—it made him mad. I broke up the commotion. That evil look you gave me sent chills through my body."

"Yeah, my feelings were hurt."

"That didn't stop you though."

"Nope, if anything it made me try harder. I tried to explain to you that I wasn't that type of guy, but I refused to allow a dude to disrespect me. I asked him what his problem was."

"Do you remember what happened when you started explain why you and Draco were about to fight?"

Rhizome flashed a boyish grin. "Yep. You leaned in and kissed me while I was talkin'. With yo' lil fast ass."

"I was being fast, wasn't I?"

"You sure was. I was in shock. I didn't know what to say. I just stood there looking stupid. You messed my mind up with that kiss and then ran off to practice. When I made it back to the locker room where the guys were, I told them about the incident and preceded to tell them what you had done. As each one of them looked at each other, they were able to see I "hooked" all because of a kiss."

"When I got out of practice that evening, I thought you would be waiting for me, but when I didn't see you, I assumed my kiss had scared you off. I was about to get on the bus and then you pulled up in a smooth mint green 1965 Chevy mustang. It was beautiful. I mesmerized."

"Yeah, that was my dad's old car. He loved it. I loved it too. I begged him to let me use it. At first, he said, *no*. Then I told him about how I needed to impress this new girl I'd met. He felt sorry for me and let me drive it. Told me he'd kill me if it came back with one scratch on it."

"You blew the horn to get my attention and asked if you could carry her home," Malady said. "I was scared to get in at first, but I said to myself: *what the hell*, and got in."

"I'm glad you did."

"So am I. You went on and on about how you weren't a violent guy. And how you didn't want me to think that all you wanted from me was sex. You said you wanted to get know me better."

"I was smooth, wasn't I? I blew you away with all that game I was kickin'."

"Whatever. That was my senior year and I wanted to be the envy of prom. I knew I could with you on my arm."

"It was the beginning of the year, and I asked you right then and there if I could take you to your prom."

"Yes, you did." Malady held out her hand. Rhizome grabbed it. "And I said, yes, before you could change your mind."

"I know you are glad you did because look at us now," Rhizome said pridefully. "You ended up saying yes when I asked you to marry me."

"Getting married is something that my parents believed in and I believed in it as well."

'Well, if you believed in it, you sure didn't act like it. You kept grilling me with questions."

"That's because I wanted to know if you were serious. I needed to know if you really loved me."

Rhizome laughed. "I remember when you asked me that I said, 'Do we need to be in love to get married?' You looked at me like I had three heads."

"I sure did. I wanted to know if you really thought it was okay for us to get married at such a young age. I remember staring into my bedroom mirror and wondering if I was old enough to take care of everything that is going on in my life and a husband too. Tell me, Rhizome, what was it about me that you loved and why did you want to marry me?"

Rhizome thought for a moment and then said, "I just knew early on that you'd make a good wife and good mother." He looked at her and smiled. "Based on the way things turned out, I think I was one hundred percent right in both cases."

Chapter 6

L iberty walked in the house and could tell at a glance that she'd interrupted something special happening between her parents. She and Malady locked eyes. The matriarch shook her head just enough to signal to Liberty that it was time for her to mention anything about their Thanksgiving plans. Liberty caught the hint. She walked over and gave both parents a hug.

"Hey, daddy."

"Hey, baby. You're home early."

"Yeah. I finished my work early and decided to take the rest of the day off. I'm surprised to see you here this early in the day."

"Yeah, the guys have everything under control. I decided to shut it down early."

"For a change," Malady said.

"I'm hot and sticky. I'm going to go take a shower."

Liberty was the only one child who still lived at home. She hadn't had a steady boyfriend in years, and as a result, had no kids. The lack of a personal life made it easy for her to live with her parents. She slept in the same bedroom that she had from the day they brought her home from the hospital as a newborn.

After washing off the day's filth, she returned to the living room. "What's for dinner?"

"I made some red beans and rice, and fried some chicken. I was about to fix your daddy a plate. Do you want some?"

"Yes, ma'am."

Malady prepared Rhizome's plate. Liberty brought the plate of food and his drink over to him. He was so engrossed in the ballgame that he didn't look at her when she delivered it.

"Thanks, baby."

"You're welcome, daddy."

Liberty returned to the kitchen and sat down at the table along with her mother.

"Did you contact your sisters and brother?" Malady asked.

"Yes ma'am. They're all coming."

They spoke in whispered tones.

"You sure?"

"I'm sure that they all said they'd be here. I can't guarantee they're all going to stick to their word." Liberty scooped up a few beans and rice and shoved it into her mouth. "Don't only one I'm kind of worried about is Natal."

"Yeah, that girl is about as predictable as the weather," Malady said. "Keep in contact with her. If she starts to sound like she's going to back out let me know and I'll call her."

"Yes, ma'am."

Liberty finished off her meal and returned to the living room. By that time, Rhizome had finished his meal and Malady was sitting in her favorite chair again.

While the three of them engaged in conversation about varying topics, a commercial depicting to teenagers going to a prom came on.

"Honey, do you remember our prom?"

Rhizome smiled. "How could I forget." He flashed a devilish grin and winked.

Liberty stuck her fingers into her ears. "No, no, no…I do not want to hear about the nasty things you two did after the prom."

Malady chuckled. "We weren't too bad. It was the best time of my young life. You should've seen how handsome your daddy looked that evening."

"I spent the whole day getting ready," Rhizome said. "Haircut. Got my dad's car washed and detailed. All so I could make a good impression."

"You blew her away daddy?"

"You know I did," Rhizome said cockily. "She had already hinted a few months earlier that she wouldn't have a curfew after the prom and that she wanted to do something different. I decided to rent out the Putt-Putt golf course. She was excited about that."

"I was. None of my friends had dates who did anything that thoughtful for them," Malady said. "Most teens act like after the prom it is mandatory for you to have sex, but with us, sex was the last thing on our minds."

"Speak for yourself," Rhizome said.

"Daddy!"

"I'm kidding…partially. Seriously, I was just happy that we were together. Just being in each other's company was the most exciting thing for me."

"That excitement didn't last long," Malady said. "I found out later that night that he was softening me up to tell me he was going away to school."

"Really. Daddy, I never knew you went away to college."

"Yeah, I was a pretty good football player in high school. Good enough to earn a full scholarship to the University of Tennessee. I was scared to tell your mother."

"Why?"

"Because I wondered if she would start dating someone else. Your mama was a fox."

"A fox?" Liberty asked and chuckled.

"Yeah…that's what we used to call the pretty girls back in the day. Your mama had all kinds of boys checking her out."

"Stop it," Malady said and blushed.

"It's the truth," Rhizome continued. "I wondered if she would be in love with me."

"Did you tell her while y'all played Putt-Putt golf?"

"No. I got cold feet. I waited until we went out to eat after our graduation. We went out to eat."

"I could tell something was bothering him, so I kept pressing him to tell me what was on his mind."

"While we ate, I finally built up the nerve to tell her I got a scholarship offer out of state. I wanted to be the one to tell her before the rumors got out."

"What did you say, mama?"

"I didn't know what to say. I was in a daze. Your dad snapped his fingers in front of my face to get my attention. I looked at him and said, 'That's great baby, congratulations.'"

"I knew she didn't mean it," Rhizome said. "She didn't even look me in the eyes when she said it. I remember feeling sick to my stomach at that moment. I knew that I might have lost the love of his life."

"What happened?" Liberty asked. She was tuned in to the story like it was a movie on the Lifetime channel.

Malady and Rhizome shared knowing grins.

"Your daddy was afraid he'd lost me, and I was sitting there thinking the same thing—I thought I was about to lose him. I decided to give him the most precious thing I could offer—myself."

"Mama!" Liberty exclaimed and put her hand over her mouth.

"I know, I know…that was a dumb thing to do, but I was young and in love, and when you're immature you make bad decisions. We were much too young for all that, but that's what happened."

"As much as you pounded into my head to not have sex until I was married," Liberty said.

Malady nodded in agreement. "You're right. I did pound that into your head. I'll spare you all the details of what happened that night."

"Good, because I don't want to know," Liberty said.

"I will tell you this much because it was so romantic. Your daddy rented the penthouse suite at a hotel."

"Daddy, you were a teenager. Where did you get that kind of money?"

"I cut a lot of yards and saved every dime I earned," Rhizome said and laughed.

"When we got to the suite, he told me to put on a mask. He said he had something special planned for me. So, I put on the mask. He led me into the room."

"Mama, I don't want to hear this," Liberty said and stuck her fingers in her ears again.

"Aww child, relax. I'm not going to tell you anything nasty. I'm telling you this much because I want you to know how romantic your father was, and what you should expect from any man courting you."

Liberty removed her fingers from ears. "Okay, go ahead…I'm listening."

"I could smell the roses as we walked into the hotel room. Your daddy told me to remove my mask. You'll never believe what was waiting for me."

"What?" Liberty asked.

Malady held up her hand and wiggled her fingers. "This beautiful three caret diamond ring."

"Daddy! How could you afford this at that age?"

"Like I said, I saved every dime I made doing all kinds of odd jobs. One of the places I worked at was the pawn shop. An old white man owned it. Mr. Greenburg. I told him my plans and he gave me a deal on a ring that had been pawned. The owner never returned to get it. I put down two hundred dollars and Mr. Greenberg sat that ring to the side. He worked me like a slave—I took out trash, mopped the floors, even worked behind the counter as a salesman on some days. Trust me, he made me earn that ring—he didn't just give it to me."

"Your daddy got down on one knee and said—"

"Will you marry me?" Rhizome blurted out.

"I didn't know at the time that he had already gotten permission from my mother," Maldady said. "My mother wanted me out of the house, so she didn't object."

"What did you do when daddy proposed?"

"I screamed, 'Yes! Yes! Yes!' Your daddy lifted me up…I'll end the story there."

"Thank you," Liberty said. "Y'all should be ashamed of yourselves."

"I'm not ashamed," Rhizome said. "That was the night the love of my life committed to me," he looked at Liberty, "and my first child was conceived."

Chapter 7

Liberty went into the kitchen and grabbed a bowl of ice cream. She brought Rhizome a bowl as well—Malady declined.

"Malady, you used to always eat ice cream after super. Your eating habits have changed. You feelin' okay?"

Liberty looked at her mother. It was clear to her that her father was still unaware of the severity of his wife's condition. Of course, he knew that she had been diagnosed with cancer—that was a fact he'd been aware of for three years. But he thought she was still in remission. She wasn't. In fact, the cancer had returned with vengeance.

Differing emotions swirled inside of Liberty. On one hand, she felt guilty that her father was being kept in the dark. After all, as a husband, he deserved to know what was going on with his wife. But, Liberty also had the utmost respect for her mother. It wasn't her place to usurp her mother's plans. She intended to respect her judgment on this one.

In an effort to change the subject, Liberty tossed out another question to the couple.

"So, I was born out of wedlock," Liberty said.

"No, you were born out of love," Rhizome corrected.

"She was born out of love, but you need to tell the truth and shame the devil," Malady said. "We hit a rough patch after all of that."

"What do you mean?" Liberty asked.

Malady looked at Rhizome and asked, "You wanna tell her?"

Rhizome shook his head. "I'm eatin' my ice cream. You tell her."

"Okay. I will."

"Tell me what?"

"A month passed and my pregnancy tests all came back negative. I told your dad I wasn't pregnant. He took the scholarship and went off to school. I was happy for him. Besides, I had my own life to worry about. I started going to Hendersonium Community College, and they had a pretty good basketball team. I wanted to make that team, so that's where I put all my focus and energy.

"Once the tryouts started, I started to feel odd. I called your daddy and told him my concerns. I had already done one of those pregnancy tests where you pee on the stick. It was negative, so it didn't make sense to me why I was feeling sick."

"I told her she was being paranoid," Rhizome said with a mouth full of ice cream. "I thought she was trying to break up with me."

"How did you come to that conclusion?" Liberty asked.

"Exactly!" Malady said. "All of these years later, and I still don't understand how he came to that conclusion. He started implying that I was seeing someone else."

Rhizome shrugged. "I guess I was a little paranoid too."

"Well, his paranoia led to us arguing. Matter of fact, it made us have one of the ugliest fights we've ever had. We broke up because of it."

"Daddy!"

Rhizome looked ashamed.

"I was a little hothead back then," Malady said. "I told him I don't need no man who can't trust me. I started accusing him of messing with one of the girls that was always flirting with him."

"Some girl was trying to push up on you daddy?"

"Child, all the girls wanted your daddy."

"Umm hmm," Rhizome grunted. "I was hot."

Malady rolled her eyes. "Anyway! The conversation got heated and I ended up cussing him out. And then I told him I was tired of the of the long-distance relationship."

"I kept asking her to move to Tennessee to come and be by me," Rhizome said.

"I didn't want to move there," Malady fired back. "You wanted the world to revolve around you."

Rhizome through up his hands.

"As I was saying," Malady continued, I cussed him out and told him to have a nice life, and then I hung up the phone in his face."

"Mama...no you didn't."

"I sure did. I wasn't about to chase him. He needed to be reminded that I was the one worth chasing."

"She definitely reminded me of that."

"Three months passed and your daddy and me didn't speak. However, one month after that argument when I hung up on him, I found out that I was pregnant. I wanted so badly to call him, but I knew that we had ended on such bad terms. I was also mad at myself for relying on that over-the-counter pregnancy test. Those things aren't always accurate. I should have just gone to the doctor when I first started feeling bad, and I would have known all along that I was pregnant. That was also when I learned that you can still have your cycle when you are pregnant."

"Did you break down and call daddy?"

"Not right away. I was determined to show Rhizome that I could do everything by myself."

"So, when did you finally tell this handsome man that he was going to be a daddy?"

Rhizome held out his spoon and Liberty tapped her spoon against his. There way of high-fiving without hands.

"It was July 4th and all of the festivities were beginning to happen," Malady continued. "The town was starting its celebration and even though I had no clue that Rhizome was going to be doing a surprise visit home to his mom, I knew that I had to tell his mother that I was about to have his baby.

"The picnic was schedule to start at 2:30 pm but before the picnic, I wanted to talk with Mrs. Desirous. So, without any hesitation, I picked up the phone and gave her a call. 'Good evening Mrs. Desirous, I was calling to see if we could talk before the picnic. There is something really important that I need to talk to you about before someone else talks to you.' Do you know what she said?"

"What?" Liberty asked, a spoonful of ice cream hovering inches away from her mouth while she waited to hear the rest.

"She said, 'Well Malady, if it is about the baby, I am fully aware that Rhizome is the father and I know that you are already expecting. Your mother called me a couple of months back, and explained the situation to me. She asked that I not say anything and allow you and Rhizome to work this situation out like adults. I told her that I wouldn't get involved, but before the baby was born that I was going to be by your side.'"

"Wow, grandma said that?"

"Yes, she did," Malady responded. "I was relieved to know that she was aware. However, I did apologize for not telling her when I found out and I asked for her forgiveness. She said, 'Baby, sometimes we learn from the mistakes that we make. As women we gain knowledge, respect, understanding, and dedication in the amazing strength of learning on our own. As you are about to begin this journey as a mother, you will learn that sometimes, help is always needed.' I started crying and thanked Mrs. Desirous for the advice that she had just given her. I swear, next to my own mother, I've never loved a woman as I loved your daddy's mama."

"She was special," Rhizome said.

"Yes, she was a special lady," Malady mumbled. "Anyway…back to the story. I walked to the square where the picnic was happening to see if I could find your father. I saw a tall man off in the distance. I was approaching him from behind so I couldn't see his face. I also noticed that he was talking to a girl. They were talking the way couples do, so I just kept looking around for your dad. As I got closer to the tall guy talking to the pretty girl, I realized that it was your father."

Rhizome put his spoon in his owl and covered his face.

"Daddy!" Liberty leaned over and smacked his arm.

"When I realized it was him, I tried to turn away so that he wouldn't see me, but I was too late. 'Malady! Malady!' he started shouting. Then he grabbed my arm. I was pissed."

"What did you do, mama?"

"I'll tell you what she did," Rhizome spoke up. "She said, 'Why are you touching me? You have a whole girlfriend on your arms. I am the least of your worries'. And then she proceeded to walk off."

"I jogged home as fast as I could," Malady said. "I couldn't believe that the love of my life—and the father of my child—was standing right in front of me with someone else. I was so heartbroken and frustrated that I couldn't help but cry, cry, and cry.

"He called and called and called. I wouldn't answer the phone. That went on for around three weeks. I just couldn't bring herself to talk with him. I couldn't figure out the words to say to him about my pregnancy. I had no clue on what I would say when he drilled me with questions.

"Finally, my mother told me it was time to let him know. She said, 'You have been doing everything on your own, and he needs to know that he is about to be a father'. I knew she was right. I also knew that someday I would have to face him, but I was hoping it would be when the baby was older. After three cups of apple juice and 3 oranges later, I gathered up the strength to call him back."

"She called me and the first thing I wanted to know was when and how it happened. She didn't answer. All she wanted to talk about was the girl she saw me talking to. I told her it was a friend from school. I even admitted that we'd been intimate."

"That was the last thing I wanted to hear," Malady said.

"It has been pushing 6 months since I'd heard from you. You never called me to tell me anything."

"You're right. I didn't."

"Alright then. Don't try to make it sound like I abandoned you."

"I didn't say you did, honey."

"She didn't say that, daddy," Liberty said to reassure her dad that she understood the circumstances. "Finish, mama."

"I told him that he was the only man I'd been with. He was the only man that had my attention. I showed him that I was still wearing the ring he gave me when he asked me to marry him. I told him I couldn't believe he questioned whether it was his baby, but I would gladly do a paternity test. I told him my expected due date was September 26th. I told him that his mother already knew and he didn't have to come if he didn't want to."

"Did you go, daddy?"

"Hell yeah! I went to the next few doctors' appointments and I was there for the birth of my child. I let her know I wasn't no damn deadbeat. I wasn't about to let another many raise my child." Rhizome looked at Malady. He spoke to her as if they'd been transported back in time and the situation was happening all over again. "If you would have called and talked to me from the beginning, I would have remained by your side throughout that entire process. Malady, I thought you knew the type of man I was. I would've loved you regardless of what I had done or had been doing. I vowed from that moment to spend the rest of my life showing you, what type of man I am."

"What happened to the girl you brought to the picnic, daddy?"

"I asked him the same thing," Malady said in a sassy manner. "He was telling me all of that sweet stuff, but I wanted to know what he was going to tell the young lady that he brought to the picnic."

"I told her exactly what was happening," Rhizome said proudly. "She was well aware of you and how I felt about you. She and I are still friends to this day. But I had to let her know that I was more concerned about Malady and my soon-to-be-born baby."

"It was the final doctor's appointment, and as Rhizome always did, he drove 10 hours each time to be with me. Finally, the doctor told us that the baby was set to be due any day now and we were the happiest soon to be parents that we could be. The only problem was that your daddy was so far away, and if the baby came while he wasn't there, I knew he would be devastated. I hadn't realized that school was almost out and your daddy had already completed all his finals because he explained his situation to his instructors. He was planning to stay by my side until I gave birth to you."

"Yep. Liberty was the name we decided on after giving each other a second chance to do right," Rhizome said. "The engagement was back on, and your mom and me were beginning to be more of a family."

"Was it a hard delivery?" Liberty asked.

"Oooh child! You were the toughest out of all my kids. All I remember hearing was, 'Push! Push! Push! I started pushing with all my might. You popped out and I passed out."

Liberty burst into laughter. "Really?"

"Yep. She passed out," Rhizome said and unleashed his trademark chuckle. "I was holding her hand when it happened. When her hand went limp, I started screaming and asking the doctors why she wasn't responding. The thought of losing your mother sent me to acting crazy in that delivery room.

"The nurses rushed me out of the room and proceeded to work on Malady. About 45 minutes of working on her, the nurse came into the hallway. She saw how I was pacing, so she gave me an update. She told me it was touch and go for a while, but your mom pulled through." Rhizome looked at Malady and winked. "Your mama is a fighter. Always was." Rhizome dabbed his eyes."

"Daddy, are you crying?"

"No, baby girl, I just got something in my eyes."

Liberty looked at her mom. Malady looked at her and mouth, 'He's crying.'

Liberty smiled. To see their love affair narrated, and to see her father's visceral reaction was enough to nearly driver her to tears too.

"Your mama was so bad that they put her in ICU. Eventually, I was allowed to sit with her. I visited her in that hospital every day. When she finally opened her eyes, I cried like a baby."

"Child, I looked up and saw your daddy crying—I'm talking one of those ugly cries too. I was wondering why he was crying, and why was everybody in her room crowding her bed. He explained everything that had happened during the delivery, and begged me to not do that to him ever again.

"That was the moment…"

"The moment for what?"

"The moment I knew how much your daddy loved me." Malady paused to dab her own eyes. She took a deep breath and then continued. "I asked where my child was. Your daddy said, 'Here is the lovely Liberty'. He cradled you in his arms and then gave you to me. I was so excited to see that I had a healthy and beautiful baby girl. However, I was a little cautious on how I would be able to interact with you."

"Why?" Liberty asked.

"Because of knowing everything that had just occurred. I didn't want to hurt myself or harm you. I didn't know if I was strong enough to hold you, so I decided to just kiss and look at you while your daddy held you."

"It was six months before them folks at the hospital would let you and your mama come home," Rhizome said. He frowned as if the thought of it all still angered him." Rhizome pointed at Malady. "Tell her what happened when you finally got out of the hospital."

Malady smiled. "When they finally released me, I went to my parents house. A few days later, our daddy came over with flowers. He knelt on the side of the bed and asked, 'When are we getting married?'"

"You said, yes?" Liberty asked.

"No!" Rhizome said. "Your mama looked at me and said—"

Malady cut him off. "I looked at him and said…it's about damn time!"

Chapter 8

Liberty went to bed that night with a better appreciation for her parents' relationship and their honesty. They could've sugarcoated the story, but they didn't. They kept it real and she appreciated that.

Liberty wouldn't dare say it to her parents, but a part of her was a little jealous of what they had. She secretly felt that their heavy-handed approach to raising her robbed her of potentially meeting someone who could give her the life they had.

While she lie in bed trying to go to sleep, she reflected on her life.

Because Liberty was their first, Rhizome and Malady used her as an example for the other children.

Rhizome knew that he had to be hard on Liberty because Liberty would be the beginning of how their children would be. That treatment persisted all through high school. It became so overbearing that Liberty only applied to out of state colleges just so she could get out of her parents' house.

When Liberty was in her freshmen year of college, she knew that she needed to do all that she could in order to have good grades. In high school she was an A and B student because Rhizome had always been hard on her, but she didn't really them to motivate her to excel in college. Making the Dean's list enabled her to qualify for scholarships to help pay for tuition and books. She also knew that her siblings were paying attention to how she performed. Being a good role model for Prosperous, Antenatal, and Dynamo was extremely important to her. It was her way of showing them that they could be anything that they wanted to be if they had put their hearts and minds to it.

All throughout high school, Liberty never dated. Rhizome was too strict on her and Malady never disagreed with how Rhizome treated the kids. She knew that he loved them and the decisions that he made were for the best interest of their children.

Getting exposed to the freedom of college life has a weird effect on some people. Since Liberty had been sheltered her entire life, her natural response to all the freedom she now had was to become wild.

By the fourth month of school, Liberty was partying all the time, not going to class, and spending most of her days working at restaurants. She was more focused on getting money than an education and her grades reflected that.

Rhizome sensed the change in his oldest daughter. When her grades came home two months later, they had dropped to D's and F's.

Rhizome called to speak with her, but received no answer. He then called her dorm room because he assumed that she was sleeping. To his surprise, Liberty still didn't answer. At this point, Rhizome was beginning to worry. He called campus security to notify them that he had been looking for his daughter and was unsuccessful with getting in touch with her. The police informed him that they would go by the dorms and see if she was there, and if she wasn't, they would notify all necessary parties.

Six weeks passed before Rhizome heard from Liberty. When they finally spoke, he told her, that he was disappointed with her grades and that he needed her to call him every day to so that he would know that she was all right.

Liberty was so frustrated that she just told her father okay. She had to learn how to deal with the idea that even being grown she was still a kid in their eyes.

Months passed and Liberty couldn't keep up with school and work. She knew that one had to go, but figuring out which one she had to let go was the hardest decision that she would ever make.

Malady made it clear that she would support whatever decision she made, so Liberty dropped out of college to pursue other avenues within her life. She went to TWISBPS School of Technology where she received her Certification in Radiology. As a certified Radiology Technician, she was able to get a great paying job at the hospital. This would be the first of many life-changing moments for Liberty.

Liberty had been employed three months when a handsome, tall, and dark young man by the name of Bumper, came into the radiology room to have x-rays on his leg completed.

Upon entering the room, Liberty knew that she had to figure out how to get Bumper's attention. As she instructed him on how to stand, and where to place and how to face, she could smell the lovely fragrance of the cologne he wore. It was just his cologne. Everything about him made her body numb. Still, she had no clue how to get his attention.

In high school she didn't date. In college she didn't date. She was totally inexperienced. This would be the first of real dates if she could ever get him to pay attention to her.

As Bumper was about to leave, he paused, turned around, and asked Liberty, "What is your name and would it be alright if I could get your number?"

Liberty was in so much shock that she couldn't speak or say anything; however, she ended up having to follow him into the hall to give him the information that he asked for.

Nearly a month later, Bumper still had not contacted her. No one else caught her attention because Liberty believed that once she spoke with someone or that she saw someone, especially as handsome as Bumper and he was interested in her, then she was supposed to be with him. However, she didn't understand why Bumper had not called and she was about to lose interest in him.

April 29th would be a day that Liberty would never forget. Bumper Slipmission finally gave her a call.

"Hey, Liberty. This is Bumper. Do you remember me?"

"Yes, I remember you. I should be asking you if you remembered me. You never called."

"I know. I've been busy. And then when I wasn't busy, I couldn't find your number. I tore my house up today and found your number. So, now I'm calling you."

"What do you want?" Liberty asked, trying to sound uninterested when she really wanted to jump for joy.

"I was wondering if you are busy t. If not, I'd like to take you to dinner and then maybe we could catch a movie."

Liberty smiled and responded, "As long as I am back home by midnight. I have to be at work on time tomorrow. My job is important to me. I'm new here and I don't want to come in late."

Bumper smiled. "Don't worry. I'll make sure you are home before midnight."

While on their first date, Bumper explained to Liberty what he did for a living as well.

"I have a confession," Bumper said.

"I'm all ears," Liberty replied.

"I live a dangerous lifestyle."

"What does that mean?"

"Just what I said. I'm considered by some people to be a real dangerous guy. I know you're a good girl and I should not pursue you, but I am really attracted to you."

Bumper was right—Liberty was a good girl. But what didn't know was that she was tired of being a good girl. She wanted to check out life on the bad side for a while.

As Bumper was leaving to take Liberty home, she asked if he would take her by his place so she would know where he lived. Without hesitation he drove by his house.

"This is my main house."

"How many houses do you have?"

Bumper smirked and said, "A few."

"Can I look inside," Liberty asked.

"Sure." Bumper parked and took inside to give her a tour. "I'm telling you up front, if you go in there you're going to be in trouble!"

"Is that supposed to scare me?"

Bumper didn't know that Liberty had a plan of her own. As innocent as she looked, she was just as naughty as well.

"Do you live alone?" Liberty asked.

"Yep. Just me. I don't do roommates. I like my privacy."

He took her to different parts of the house. The last room that he showed her was the bedroom. As they entered, Liberty proceeded to direct Bumper to the end of the bed and threw him on top of the bed.

"What are you doing?" Bumper asked.

"Shhh," Liberty hissed.

She proceeded to undress him and finally completed the task that she intended when entering the house. Bumper was much surprised, but wore the happiest of smiles.

They made love for hours. It was the best experience of her life. She had every intention of sexing him, but not staying the night.

Liberty glanced over at the clock and saw that it was nearly midnight. Bumper was sound asleep. She didn't want to wake him, but she didn't want to stay either.

Was I too aggressive? Did I move too fast? Will he think I'm a whore? Will he think I do this all the time?

She was having so many wild thoughts that she was making herself miserable.

Fortunately, he rolled over and looked at her.

"Did I doze off?"

"A little bit," Liberty whispered.

Bumper looked at the clock. "Oh shit, it's almost midnight. Come on, let me take you home."

When the hours turned to days and Bumper still hadn't called, Liberty assumed she'd gotten her answer—she'd been too forward.

What Liberty didn't know was that when Bumper dropped her off that morning, two officers pulled him over and searched his car when he was going back home. They planted drugs and a weapon in his car, and arrested him for having these items within his possession. The officers were so foolish because they denied him the right to counsel, which also violated more of his rights. Nevertheless, Bumper continued to wear a smile, as he was being booked in and arrested.

Three months passed before Liberty heard or seen Bumper again. On July 13th a bouquet of yellow, red, and white roses were delivered to her at work. The card attached to the flowers read:

"Please forgive me for not being around; forgive me for not being able to call or come by to see you. I have been in jail and while my rights were violated, I thank those officers for treating me that way. If you can find it in your heart to forgive me, meet me at Windsorrange Park @ 5:45pm."

Even though Liberty thought about ignoring the gesture, deep down she wanted an explanation of what happened and why Bumper dropped off the face of the Earth for so long. She decided to take a chance to see what his explanation would be so she went to meet him.

The clock struck 5:00 pm and she needed to get home to take a shower and change clothes. She had 45 minutes to meet the man she once considered to be *the one*. She wasn't buying the story that he was in jail because she had no proof of that. She wanted answers and she was determined to get those answers.

As she entered Windsorrange Park she noticed a slender, sexy, well dressed young man standing near the bench that Bumper asked her to meet him. She couldn't make out if it was him or not because the last time she saw Bumper, he had a few extra pounds. On this day, his body was skinnier than the man she first met.

When she approached the bench, she got a whiff of the cologne and immediately knew that he had to be Bumper.

"Hello Bumper."

They hugged. Liberty didn't want to release her grip, but she managed to.

Bumper could sense something had changed with Liberty. "What is wrong? Why do you have such a glow about you? Why does it look like you have added a few more pounds?"

Liberty was so furious with Bumper that she asked him, "Why did you call me? What is it that you want from me? You drop off the face of the Earth for three months and then suddenly reappear. You claim that you were in jail, but I have yet to see proof of that and you look like skin and bones." She paused to catch her breath. "Bumper, if you don't like me just say it and let me go on with my life."

Bumper was completely speechless, because a simple meet and greet turned into the worse conversation that he could have hoped for.

"To answer your questions, I didn't want anything from you, I just wanted to see you and tell you why I hadn't called. I wanted you to know that those months that I had to sit in jail gave me time to think and realize that I don't want to be in the game any longer. I want more out of life."

The moment he stopped talking, Liberty blurted out, "I'm pregnant! And before you ask, it *is* yours."

"How are the two of you doing?"

"The doctors told m that the pregnancy will probably be a complicated one, and that I may have to be placed on bed rest at some point."

Liberty, however, did not care because she was determined to have this baby no matter what. As Bumper realized that he was about to be a father for the first time, he knew that he had to do something to provide the best life for this child.

Bumper pulled her in for a hug. While her face rested on his chest he whispered, "Don't worry. I'm going to take care of you and my child."

Another two weeks passed before Liberty saw Bumper again. They had decided to date and get to know each other. They knew that they were having a child together, and knew that they needed to communicate with each other on how they would raise this child.

One evening, Bumper came to Liberty's apartment for dinner and talked about the things that they needed to do when it came time for the baby to arrive.

Liberty noticed Bumper appeared drowsy.

"You look sleepy," Liberty said. "You want to spend the night?"

"You don't mind?"

"No. But I want you to sleep on the couch."

"That's fine," Bumper said, to tired to put up a fight. "I just need to rest for a few. I haven't been sleeping well and I feel like it's catching up to me."

Around three o'clock that morning, Liberty screamed. Bumper leapt to his feet and ran to her bedroom. When he entered the room, he saw Liberty lying in a pool of blood. The baby was lost.

Chapter 9

The days raced by faster than a sprinter during the Olympics. Thanksgiving eve was upon them and the dinner preparation started. Cake bowls were filled with mix. A turkey fatter than a small dog sat on the countertop, frozen hard enough to punch a hole through the wall. Malady moved around the kitchen like a drill sergeant, moving pots and pans to and froe while barking orders at Liberty.

Dynamo was the first of the out-of-town kids to arrive. Military life looked good on him. He was tall and as handsome as always. There was a confidence in his gait, but that confidence dwindled when he arrived home. When he stepped into his parents' house, the negative memories that drove him away came flooding back and made his head throb.

When he was younger, he was clumsy. If he even looked at stairs, he would fall and break a bone.

As a kid, Rhizome was hell bent on his only boy being the sole heir to the family lawn service. He never knew or believed that one-day Dynamo would choose to go into the service.

Dynamo was the captain of the football team, the best drummer in the band, the point guard for the basketball team, yet the most unpopular kid in the school. Back then, Rhizome was the basketball coach and the most difficult math teacher in the school. Kids always teased Dynamo on being nerdy.

It might seem unbelievable that a boy so talented would be so unpopular. It was because of the situation he found himself in.

Dynamo was determined to have straight A's in school. No one knew, but his father was harder on him than any other student in the school. Rhizome would often say, "You are a product of me; therefore, and you will not embarrass or make our family look bad."

Dynamo knew that he had no choice but to be the best leader he could be and excel in all his classes. Because, despite being in high school, he was more likely to get a beating when he got home.

Dynamo's weekends were never as normal as you might assume they would be. On Friday's, if there was no game, he had to go to work. Whether it was dealing with the family business or household chores, he had to make sure that it was completed.

Dynamo always confided in his younger sister, Antenatal, on how life in the "Rhizome" house was hard. Antenatal explained that Rhizome was only helping him to learn how to be a man, and that in the long run he would be very content with how hard their daddy was on him. Then again, that still didn't prevent Dynamo from complaining about how he had to make sure that he was always on point with grades, sports, and household responsibility.

Striving to be the best sister that she could, Antenatal just sat, and listened and allowed Dynamo to vent. Still, Dynamo didn't realize that Rhizome was preparing him for the world and being responsible, as he would soon enter the world.

By Dynamo's junior year, he was social outcast. He had no idea that the most popular girl in school wanted to date him.

Dynamo, was wondering who was going to be his date for prom. Football season was over and basketball season was beginning. He knew that he couldn't ask his father for money, because he had wasted countless weekends practicing and no time working.

Rhizome was a very serious man; Dynamo knew that asking for money would be out of the question. Nevertheless, Dynamo really wanted to go to the dance, so going against his better judgement he asked his father if he could have some money to look nice for the Prom. To his surprise, his father was more than excited to buy him a suit for Prom; however, he had to ask the question that made the conversation odd.

"Who is the lucky young lady that you are taking to Prom?" Rhizome asked.

Dynamo immediately went into defense mode before he knew it. "Do you always have to have a girl to go to Prom? Can I just go by myself?"

Rhizome knew that something was wrong because Dynamo never spoke to him in that tone.

"Malady, what is wrong with Dynamo?" Rhizome asked. "He finally asked if I would assist him with going to the prom, but when asked if he had a date, he snapped at me."

"Well Rhizome, I have no clue if you realize or not, but Dynamo is very unpopular. He is talked about on a daily basis because he seems to be too smart. Kids tease him about everything that he does and even blame his success on the fact that you are a teacher at the school. They very rarely speak to him even though he has all of the titles to be the most popular kid in the school."

"Malady, why has no one told me what is going on with Dynamo?"

"Dynamo feels like if someone tells you, you will only get onto him about it and take out the anger and frustration of people talking about him on him. He just feels like if he can get through these next two years without any incident then you will be more than happy and won't be on his back so much."

As Rhizome realized that he was always on Dynamo's case he sat down to ponder about all the issues that he assumed Dynamo was facing.

"Antenatal, does a guy always have to have a date in order to go to the prom?" asked Dynamo.

"Only if he is looking to spend money!" laughed Antenatal. "Why do you ask?"

"Well, daddy just asked me if I had a date to Prom, and I asked him, why was it so important for me to have a date? I may be grounded for my actions, but he doesn't understand what all I have to go through at school." Dynamo sat on the bed. "I am always ragged on by the boys on the team because of my name, and no girls that I have ever asked out want to date me. Is there something wrong with me Antenatal? And don't just say, *no*, because you are my sister. I want to know the truth is there something wrong with me?

Antenatal looked at Dynamo and said, "There is only something wrong with you if you believe that there is something wrong with you! I have told you over and over again, you are the most handsome, intelligent, and talented guy I have ever known—even though you are my brother. Dynamo, you stand 6'5" and about 325 lbs. You have dark brown eyes with cute baby lips and you are the geekiest person I have ever met. You are very respectful when it comes to girls, and you are always willing to help anybody whenever you can. Any girl who doesn't see that and can't respect that doesn't deserve to date my big brother. Now that is some truth for you."

As much as Dynamo loved hearing his sister talk about him and try to make him feel better, he still wondered why he was so unpopular. Why was he always talked about at school? Why couldn't he ever find a girl to go out with him? As these questions ran through his mind he listened to Antenatal as she continued to talk.

Finally, it was Friday, two weeks before Prom and even though Dynamo still had no date, he wondered if he could find someone. Being that he was the captain of the football team and the best dunker on the basketball team, he had always had his eye on Shanty.

Shanty was the captain of the cheerleading squad and the most popular girl in school. She was shaped like a Coca-Cola bottle and was very respected among the *cool* crowd. However, she was extremely smart and got nothing less than an A on all her work.

Dynamo, wondered if she would like to accompany him to the prom. Over the course of the week, he would leave cute little notes in Shanty's locker with sweet little poems. He would stand around the corner to see if she would read the notes as they fell from her locker when she opened it.

Shanty would pick them up and as she opened them, she turned to each side to see who had left the notes. Due to her not seeing anyone she proceeded to open the note and read what it said. One of the poems went something like this:

"Your mind is like a flower; each day it blossoms more. The way that you speak brings life and joy ever more. How can someone as beautiful as you not see thee. How much you mean to me!"

As Shanty read over the poem, she couldn't help but smile and again look around to see if she could tell who had left it. Dynamo still stood behind the wall where Shanty did not see him. So, after three days of getting poems, Shanty decided to come up with a plan to see just who was leaving her notes in the locker.

She explained to her mom that she had a student council meeting early in the morning and she needed to be at school by 7:15 am. So, the next morning, Shanty and her mom woke up, she quickly got Shanty to school. However, this time, she beat Dynamo to school and was able to stand around the corner to see exactly who was leaving the notes.

As Dynamo made it to campus, he looked around before approaching Shanty's locker. He glanced around the hall to see if anyone was looking and to his surprise no one was paying attention. He took out the note and dropped it into the locker.

Dynamo had always timed her entrance into the building and as he was about to run and hide around the corner, he bumped into Shanty. He looked in shocked and amazed and finally mustered up the ability to speak.

"Good morning Shanty, how are you doing today?"

Shanty looked and smiled at Dynamo as she responded, "Good morning to you as well Dynamo, I am fine, thanks for asking."

As she walked past Dynamo, he couldn't help but wonder if she was aware that he had placed a note in her locker. As he snuck behind the corner, and glanced at her as she opened her locker; he waited to see what her reaction would be. This time, the note was a little different and she looked around to see that he was looking at her from the corner. The note read:

"For the longest, I have been admiring who you are! I have wondered, what it would be like to date someone like you? I only have one question: Would you do the honor of accompanying me to Prom?"

Dynamo could feel his emotions swirling. The moment had arrived. The girl of his dreams was reading another one of his poems, and what was more important, he could tell she knew he was the writer. There would be more need to hide behind corners or sneak into her locker. Their romance would be acknowledged and put on display for the world to see.

Shanty read the poem slowly. When she was finished, she looked in his direction. Feeling empowered, Dynamo stepped into the hallway. In his mind, he envisioned her running toward him and jumping into his arms. They'd stand their kissing until other students saw. The word would get out. They'd be a couple.

Unfortunately, life doesn't always imitate art. Shanty's face scrunched like she'd bit into a lemon. She crumpled the poem and tossed into the garbage can near her locker.

At that same moment, Derek Jones, the star running back on the football team approached her. She flashed the smile that Dynamo thought she was going to give him. Derek opened his arms. Shanty wrapped her arms around his waist. They kissed until other students entered the hallway. The word got out—Shanty and Derek were the new hottest couple in the school.

Chapter 10

Antenatal's sputtering Toyota Camry could be heard as it made its way up the block. The breaks squealed like a stuck pig as she pulled into her parent's driveway. She sat there for a moment, feeling the weight of embarrassment draped around her neck.

Liberty and Dynamo were on the porch talking when she arrived. There was no way to know what they were saying, but she could tell that they were whispering about her from their facial expressions and the way they went from animated to nearly stone-faced.

This disturbed Antenatal more than the awful sound of her car. She and Liberty were sisters by blood, but rivals by stature. This wasn't the way Liberty saw their relationship, but it was certainly the viewpoint Antenatal held.

The subtle competition between the two sisters started during Antenatal's freshman year in highs school. Because of all the attention Liberty received from their parents, Antenatal always wanted to demonstrate that she was smarter than her oldest sister. She convinced Rhizome and Malady to send her to what she called the "best" high school—one where she played basketball, and became one of the most popular students in the school. Truth be told, she wasn't nearly as talented as Liberty, but in her twisted mind, she felt as if she was.

What Antenatal was undeniably better at was getting away with things. Before they went to bed at night, they were supposed to wash the dishes and wipe down the countertops, she found ways to get out of doing that. Whenever their mother needed someone to go to the corner store, she got out of doing that. And the one thing she was definitely better at doing than Liberty was finding ways to get out of the house at night to sneak around with boys.

One day, Antenatal decided that she would push her luck and see how far she could really get away with things. She wanted to do something that Liberty could only dream of while in high school; she wanted to date.

Due to Antenatal being the most popular girl in school, she found out that the second most popular boy seemed to be really attracted to her. While washing he face one morning, she looked into the bathroom mirror and mumbled, "I'm only a freshman, but if I dated a junior, that would put me even higher on the social map than I have ever expected."

Since Antenatal craved popularity more than good grades, the thought seemed logical to her. From that moment on, she set her sights on landing an older boy.

While talking to her best friend, Chimera, she learned that a popular boy named, Risqué, wanted to date her.

"He asked me for your phone number the other day, but I told him I needed to talk to you first," Chimera said. "Do you want me to give it to him?"

"Yes!" Antenatal shouted.

Chimera laughed. "He really likes you. He asked me if you were dating anyone right now."

"What did you tell him?"

"I told him, no." Chimera said. "He also asked me if your father was strict—wanted to know if he would allow you to go out with him?"

Everyone that went to school there was already aware that Rhizome was hard on Liberty and that she couldn't date until she was in college. But no one knew whether Antenatal was under the same restrictions because he acted more carefree and unbridled.

"I told him that you might be able to go out with him, but he should let me come talk to you first before he approached you."

"Why'd you tell him that?" Antenatal asked.

"To make him sweat a little. Risqué is used to all these girls around here sweatin' him all the time. He needs to put in some work to date my best friend." Chimera waved dismissively. "Girl relax, that boy is crazy about you. He ain't goin' nowhere."

Around lunchtime, Chimera ran into Antenatal after gym class.

"Natal! Giiiirrrll, come here. I need to tell you something."

"What?"

"Risqué can't stop talking about you. That boy is practically begging me to get you to date him. He even offered to hook me up with his cute homeboy, Jeffrey."

"You're lyin'!"

"No, I'm not. He wants to know if you would sneak out the house to come meet him?"

"What did you tell him?"

"I told him, yes."

"Why'd you tell him that before you talked to me?"

"Because he's bringing Jeffrey. They're going to meet us at the park."

My Daddy will kill me if he found out I was sneaking out to meet a boy, Antenatal thought. *Then again, maybe he won't be too mad. He has seemed more laid back since Liberty is getting ready to go off to college and Prosperous is not far behind her. He knows times are changing, so he needs to loosen up a little. Maybe he'll give me an opportunity to date."*

As Antenatal listened to Chimera talk about the conversation, she had with Risqué she couldn't help, but think of ways in which she could make things work even if her father wouldn't allow her to date him. Sure, she could sneak out of the house, but that might prove to be more trouble than it was worth. In the end, she decided to be honest about her desires and ask her father if she could date.

Later that night, Rhizome was sitting on the sofa watching television. No one was around, so Antenatal seized the moment.

"Daddy, can I talk to you about something?"

"Yeah, what's on your mind, Natal?"

She sat down next to him on the sofa.

"I know that you don't normally do this and you may even say, no, but I would be foolish if I didn't at least try and ask you."

"Ask me what, Natal? Spit it out. My show is about to come on."

"Can I please go on a date with Risqué?"

"Risqué," Rhizome said, conjuring up the boys face. "Yeah, I know him. he's a good kid. Makes good grades. I don't mind you going out on a date with, but you must keep your grades up."

Antenatal started clapping like she'd won a prize. He leapt into her father's arms and wrapped her arms around his neck.

"Alright, alright," Rhizome said, struggling to unlock her arms from around his neck, "don't kill me." He held her at arm's length and looked into her eyes. "But you must promise that you will be responsible if I am allowing you to start dating."

"I will, Daddy."

"You know what I'm talking about, don't you?"

"Yes, Daddy. No sex."

"That's right," Rhizome said. "Y'all are too young for all that."

Antenatal kissed her father on the cheek and ran out of the room before he had a chance to change his mind.

While in her bedroom she danced and struggled to stifle a shout. Then she thought about Liberty. She had again accomplished something her older sister couldn't.

Antenatal spent a little time posing in her bedroom mirror and gloating, and then she grabbed the phone and called, Chimera.

"Hey, Natal, what's up? Why you calling me earlier than our usual convo time? Did you talk to your dad?"

"Yeah," Antenatal replied solemnly.

Chimera assumed by the sound in her friend's voice that the conversation didn't go well. She immediately went into comfort mode.

"Don't worry about it, friend. Maybe you can talk to your mother and she'll talk to your dad for you. That's what I had to do and it worked for me. My mother softened my dad up and now I can go on dates as long as I'm home before ten o'clock at night."

"Thanks for the suggestion, but I don't know if I can do that," Antenatal said.

"Why not?"

"Because it's not necessary! My daddy said I can date Risqué!"

The two girls screamed so loud that they both had to move their phones away from their ears.

"Okay, okay," Chimera said, "lets calm down and figure out how we're going to handle Risqué and Jeffrey."

The girls giggled and plotted for the next hour. They coordinated when they would see the boys, where they would see the boys, and for how long they would see the boys.

Two days later, in the morning before class, Antenatal stood in the hallway at school in front of their wall lockers. Chimera, whose locker was next to Antenatal's, leaned with her head against the lockers while she hugged her books.

"Chimera, you act like you've never played your instrument before. Stop acting nervous. You're going to do fine."

"How do you know?" Chimera asked. "There are a lot of kinds in there who can play just as good as me."

"Chimera, it's the first band orchestra try out. Everybody is going to be nervous. I'm telling you; you're going to be amazing."

"Thanks friend. I needed to hear that."

"You're welcome." Antenatal shoved a tablet inside the locker and closed the door. "Now let's go to class before we're late."

Chimera grabbed Antenatal's arm. "Oh yeah, there's something I forgot to tell you."

"What?"

"Risqué has been looking for you."

"I ain't hard to find."

"I know. He knows that too. But he's been trying to catch you alone. He told me that every time he sees you, you're always surrounded by a lot of people."

"I can't help that," Antenatal said. "He's going to have to man up and step up."

As they headed into the band hall, Antenatal experienced that moment that every girl in the school hoped to one day have. That moment when the boy of her dreams builds up the nerves to approach her.

Risqué stood on the far wall. He spotted Antenatal and Chimera the moment they entered the room.

"Don't look now," Chimera said, "but Risqué is looking at you."

"I know, I saw him before he saw me," Antenatal replied. "I hope he comes over. I'm getting tired of waiting on him to step up."

Chimera nodded in agreement. "I'm tired too. The longer he takes to step to you, the longer it's gon' take for me to hook up with Jeffrey."

Chimera waved at Risqué and waved him over.

"What are you doing?" Antenatal whispered.

"Getting this party started," Chimera smiled and chuckled.

"What's up, Chimera?" Risqué asked.

"Nothing. Just chilling with my girl. You've been wanting to meet her, well now is your chance. Risqué this is my best friend, Antenatal."

"Hi," Risqué said.

"Hi," Antenatal replied.

Chimera smacked Risqué on the back and winked at her best friend. "Well, I'm going to let y'all talk. I'll be over here when y'all are done."

Antenatal smirked as she watched Chimera walk away. "That girl is crazy."

"Yeah, she is," Risque agreed. He glanced over his shoulder and then back at Antenatal. "I'm glad to...I mean, glad I...I mean, it's nice to finally meet you."

Antenatal almost laughed. Watching Risqué stutter was hilarious. He always walked around acting all confident. His shyness made him look cuter to her. After watching him squirm for a few seconds, she finally spoke up.

"It's nice meeting you too. I've been hoping you would come talk to me."

"Really?"

"Yes," Antenatal said and smiled.

"Cool. Let's sit right here."

They spent the entire class period whispering to each other while the band director talked. Chimera spent the entire class craning her neck to try and get a peek at them.

The next two days passed fast. During that time, Antenatal and Risqué' walked home from school together and talked on the phone for hours. They found that they had a lot in common. They agreed to go on their first date on Friday evening.

"Where are you going?" Liberty asked Antenatal.

"On a date," Antenatal replied flippantly.

"With who?"

"My new boyfriend. His name is Risqué."

"Who said you can go on a date?"

"Daddy."

Liberty leaned against the entrance to the bedroom and folded her arms. Antenatal used the mirror to spy her sister. Even though they were more than eight feet apart, she could see Liberty's bottom lip poked out.

"I don't know why daddy let you go on a date. You stay in more trouble than I've ever got into. Your grades ain't nothin' like mine. And when I wanted to go on a date he told me I couldn't."

Antenatal smiled, puckered her lips to make sure her lipstick was perfect and said, "You ain't me."

"Just proves that they've always treated you better than they treat me," Liberty said. "It doesn't matter what I do, you still get to do things that they denied me from doing."

The doorbell chimed.

"That's my date," Antenatal said. She shoved her lipstick into her pocket and sprayed some cheap perfume on her neck. "I suggest you go complain to mama. Meanwhile, I'm outta here."

Liberty fought back tears. She used the heels of her hands to dab her eyes, and then left out the room. Antenatal felt kind of bad because she knew that she received preferential treatment from their parents. She never knew why, but she saw the difference. Not only did she and Liberty see it, Dynamo saw it too.

There were times when Antenatal thought about sticking up for Liberty, but then decided not to. What if lobbying for Liberty made their parents become stricter with her? Then she would have cost her own self some privileges. Deep down, she knew it was selfish of her to not advocate for her sister, but as far as she was concerned, when it came to freedom, it was every girl for herself.

When Antenatal walked out of the house she expected to see Chimera and Jeffrey standing outside with Risque. This was supposed to be a double date, but he was standing out there all alone.

"Where is Chimera and Jeffrey?" Antenatal asked.

"Jeffrey got into it with one of his teachers," Chimera said. "The teacher called his house and told his parents. Now, Jeffrey is grounded for the rest of the month."

"Chimera didn't tell me that," Antenatal said. She looked at her cellphone. "Oh, I see that she texted me to tell me what happened while I was getting dressed."

Risqué shrugged. "So, what do you wanna do? You wanna still go out or just hook up some other time?"

Antenatal wasn't crazy about going on the date alone, but she wasn't going to let the opportunity to get out of the house—with her father's permission—go to waste.

"C'mon, let's go," she said.

Since it was only six o'clock in the evening, the sun hadn't quite clocked out for the day. The sky looked orange in the west, which was the direction they were walking.

"Antenatal, why did it take us so long to figure out that we were meant for one another?" asked Risqué.

"I think it's because some people know what they want and others don't have a clue about what they want," responded Antenatal. "For the longest time, I wanted to be with you, but I was too afraid that first, my father wouldn't want me to date anyone; and secondly, you didn't find me to be attractive."

"What? You can't be serious."

"I'm dead serious," Antenatal said. "Besides, I have always paid attention to my sister, Liberty, because believe it or not, she really sets a good example. She makes sure that we are always on top of what we are supposed to be doing and she always gives me advice when I need it."

"I heard your dad doesn't allow her to date."

"He hasn't. I don't know why he is that way, but he is. My father is a little easier on me than Liberty." Antenatal looked at her date. "Can I ask you a question?"

"Yeah."

"Why out of all of the girls in high school did you choose me to date?"

"Because I like you. I think you're cute. And I like the way you didn't just throw yourself at me. I get that a lot."

"You know you like the attention," Antenatal teased.

"No, I don't," Risqué said. "I know that a lot of people know me, but I'm really kind of shy. I prefer to play the back."

"Yeah, I kind of noticed that."

"It's the truth. I've been asking Chimera to talk to you for me because I was scared to talk to you."

"Why?"

"Because you are pretty popular too. I know a lot of guys want to talk to you. I was scared that you might crack my face if I approached you."

"Well, I didn't crack your face," Antenatal said and smiled.

"No, you didn't."

They stopped walking in the middle of the block. As they stood there looking into each other eyes, time seemed to stand still. Cars had been passing while they walked, but for those few seconds, the street was barren.

Risqué grabbed Antenatal's hand and moved closer. She moved toward him. Their eyes closed. When their lips touched, they could both hear fireworks even though it wasn't the 4th of July.

When they finished their first kiss, they smiled and held hands for the remainder of the walk to the shopping mall.

They entered the shopping mall and window shopped for nearly an hour. Antenatal went into clothing stores and held up different outfits that she thought she'd look good in. Risqué went into tennis shoe stores and tried on different pairs of tennis shoes that he couldn't afford.

"I'm hungry," Risqué said.

"Me too," Antenatal replied and rubbed her belly. "I want a hot dog."

"Let's go get something to eat at the food court." Risqué grabbed her hand and they walked to the food court. "Look at everybody staring at us."

"I've seen a couple of people from school."

"Me too," Risqué replied. "Everybody is going to be gossiping by the time we get back to school on Monday."

"Do you have a problem with that?" Antenatal asked.

Risqué smiled and kissed her knuckles. 'Do I look or act like I have a problem with it?"

They spent an hour in the food court, eating hot dogs, laughing at odd couples that passed, and talking about their respective families.

"What time do you have to be home?" Risqué asked.

"By ten o'clock," Antenatal replied shyly.

Risqué looked at his wristwatch. "It's almost nine—I should get you home. I don't want you to be late; your daddy might not let you go out with me again."

They retraced their steps home. During the walk, the conversation was just as engaging on the way back as it was when they were heading to the mall. Antenatal could feel herself relaxing and feeling completely comfortable with him.

"We are only three blocks away from my house, and I don't have to be home for another thirty minutes, lets go to the park." She pointed at a bench with a light next to it. "Let's go sit on that bench."

They sat on the bench and within seconds were kissing. Risqué pulled away.

"What's wrong?" Antenatal asked. She didn't have much practice kissing and wondered if she'd done something wrong.

"I feel like we're under a spotlight. Feels like the whole world can see us." He glanced over his shoulder. "Let's go to that bench over there."

"But it's dark over there," Antenatal said.

"Yeah, but at least we're not sitting here out in the open. What if one of your parent's friends drive past and see us kissing. They're going to tell your daddy and he'll stop you from seeing me."

Antenatal considered the scenario. The more she thought about it, the more she realized that it wasn't that farfetched.

The two lovebirds scuttled over to an area of the park where night vision binoculars would be needed to see them. They sat on the bench and resumed kissing.

"You're a good kisser," Risqué whispered.

"You too," Antenatal purred.

"You think I could be your first love?" he asked and pulled away just enough to hear her response.

Antenatal, caught up in the rapture of the moment, mumbled, "Yeah. I feel like I'm falling in love with you already."

Risque slid his hand under her shirt and fondled her breasts. Antenatal moved his hand.

"Stop."

"Why?"

"Because, I'm not ready for that."

"Do we go together?"

"Yes. But—"

"So, if we go together and you love me, then you should show me." He slid his hand under her shirt again. "I promise I won't tell anybody."

Antenatal could feel the darkness closing in on her. Here was the most popular boy in school asking her to be his girlfriend. She already admitted that she could fall in love with her, and all he wanted to do was prove it.

"You promise you won't tell anyone?" she asked.

"I promise," Natal. "You're my girl. I love you. I wouldn't do anything to hurt you."

Risqué reached inside of her shirt again. This time, Antenatal didn't stop him.

Antenatal walked through her front door with five minutes to spare. Fortunately, her mother and father weren't in the living room. Like a rat scurrying across the kitchen floor, she made a beeline for the bathroom.

Ten minutes passed before Antenatal stepped out of the bathroom. When she did, Liberty was standing in the same bedroom doorway that she stood in before Antenatal left to go on her date.

"What's wrong?" Liberty asked.

"Nothing." Antenatal brushed past her sister and went into the bedroom. Liberty followed her.

"You're lying. What happened?"

"Nothing Liberty. Leave me alone."

"Natal! Are you home?" Rhizome's voice bounced off the walls and made its way to their bedroom.

"Yes, Daddy! I got home before ten!"

Liberty closed the bedroom door and leaned on it. She crossed her arms, and with a scowl on her face, continued grilling her younger sister.

"Something happened tonight. I can tell because you're acting different."

"Nothing happened, Liberty. I just went on a date. That's all."

Liberty stared at Antenatal for a few seconds. She looked at her sister's shoes and spotted the mud stains on the sole. She noticed mud smudges on her jeans. She moved closer and knelt in front of Antenatal.

"Natal," she placed her hand on her sister's knee, "please don't tell me you did what I think you did."

67

Antenatal dropped her head and stared at her lap. While her head was facing downward, a teardrop fell and splatted on her thigh.

"He told me to prove to him that I love him," she mumbled.

Liberty glanced back to make sure the door was closed and they couldn't be heard. Satisfied that their conversation would remain trapped in that bedroom, she looked at Antenatal and grabbed her chin. She forced her little sister to look into her eyes.

"Natal, did y'all use protection?"

Antenatal stared at Liberty and without bothering to jerk away, burst into tears. Liberty leaned in and grabbed her sister. It was the first time they'd hugged each other in years, but the display of emotion showed that despite their constant bickering, neither would've wanted to be anywhere else in the world at that moment.

The flashback of the night that she lost her virginity to Risqué in the park brought back a flood of other emotions. Like the way he avoided the next week in school. The way many of his friends starting giggling whenever she walked past. How the other girls—including her so-called friend Chimera—gossiped behind her back. And the day he left her crying in the hallway when she told him she was pregnant and he said it wasn't his child.

Life from that point on had been an uphill climb. Breaking the news to her mother was hard, but watching her father cry after hearing she was pregnant was the worst. Rhizome sat in his favorite chair for more than six hours with his head hung low. His disappointment was palpable. Their relationship would never be the same.

With the car still idling, Antenatal looked out at Liberty and Dynamo. They seemed like wolves waiting to attack; or at least that's what she felt. She adjusted the rearview mirror so that she could get a better view of her ten-year-old son, Risqué Jr.—nicknamed, RJ—and stared at his innocent face.

You are the best thing I've ever done, she thought.

The child was trapped between two worlds. His father's side of the family never acknowledged him. His mother's side of the family loved him from afar, but because of the tension between Antenatal and Rhizome, the boy didn't visit often. Antenatal wasn't exactly sure why she even agreed to attend this Thanksgiving dinner, but something in her spirit told her she should.

After taking a deep breath that sounded like a deflating balloon when she exhaled, she looked at RJ through the rearview mirror and asked, "Are you ready to go see your family?"

RJ, who'd been staring out the window quietly, looked at his mother, shrugged and said, "I guess so. Are you?"

Antenatal scratched her neck and forehead. She turned off the vehicle and then craned her neck to look at her son in the backseat.

"Honestly son, I don't know if I'm ready. But if you hear me tell you to grab your things so we can leave, I don't want you to waste time. I want you to say goodbye to your grandparents, grab your things, and beat me to this car. Do you understand me?"

"Yes ma'am."

"Good. Now let's go in here and show our faces so we can eat and get back home."

Chapter 11

"Would you relax," Prosperous said she pulled out a few pieces of tissue. "You're sweating bricks."

"I know. I'm just nervous about meeting your family."

"I told you there is nothing to be nervous about. My family is just as dysfunctional as anyone else's family." She smirked. "They won't tear you up too bad."

Prosperous was always the calmest under pressure. She inherited that demeanor from her mother. From what she could recall, having a spotlight on her started as far back as when she was in the eighth grade.

She was the best clarinet player that the band had ever had, and the smartest student in her class. After following behind Liberty and Antenatal, Prosperous wanted to be better than her sisters had ever been. What Antenatal and Liberty didn't know was that Prosperous wanted to outshine both.

She was determined to do that in all ways possible. She wanted her parents to be proud of the person that she was and who she would be.

As it came time for the first semester to be over, the school announced that there would be a ceremony. The sun was spitting out a blistering heat on award day and like every other child in the Rhizome and Malady household everyone would go to represent the member of the family.

Today was Prosperous day and no one would take the spotlight of that away. The family knew, that even with Malady and Rhizome living in separate households that they are all to remain supportive of each other. As Prosperous begin to walk across the stage, the principal announced, that she had the highest average out of all the students in the entire class. Malady couldn't help but scream as Rhizome looked at the ghetto behavior that the family presented. After the ceremony, the family went out to eat and celebrated Prosperous accomplishments. However, the award ceremony was only for the first semester.

It was time for the second semester to start and Prosperous was extremely nervous about her classes. She knew that she would have to stay on top of the list from an academic standpoint and that she would have to top her sisters if she wanted to impress her parents. However, what she didn't realize is that she was making herself sick because of all the worrying that she was doing.

Malady hadn't been paying attention to Prosperous but Liberty had. Liberty could tell that Prosperous was not doing so well because she could see the signs that she once saw within herself. She knew that she needed to do something to help her baby sister understand that she didn't have to harm herself to make their parents happy.

A month into school, Prosperous brought home her progress report and to our surprise she had all B's. As she begins to hand the report to their mother she hyperventilated.

Malady, was wondering what was wrong, because to her, B's were good. However, she knew that her daughter was better than a B.

"Why are you hyperventilating?" Malady asked. "Is everything okay at school?"

Prosperous tried to explain that she was studying and doing everything that she could to keep her grades up, but sometimes when she got her exams, she would forget what were on them.

Malady called Rhizome and told him that they had to talk. Rhizome, told her that once he got off work that he would be over to speak with her.

When Rhizome got off work, he went home tired and starving. All he wanted to do was hav a cold beer and eat dinner, but he remembered that he had to talk to Malady about Prosperous.

"What's going on?" he asked.

"We need to talk about Prosperous?" Malady said.

"Can it wait?" Rhizome removed his soiled shirt and kicked off his dusty shoes. "I need some time to unwind."

"No, it can't wait." Malady handed him Prosperous progress report. "Prosperous' grades are dipping. She's better than this. I think something is wrong."

Rhizome studied the report. "Malady, the girl always does in school. She's at that awkward age in life. Her lack of focus could be the result of difficult teachers, some boy she has a crush on, or some kids giving her a hard time. Let's give her chance to bounce back before we jump all over her. I learned my lesson from being too hard on our other kids. The harder we are on them, the more they rebel."

"I hear you," Malady said, but I still think we should ask her if she is okay."

Rhizome knew that arguing with his wife was a lost cause. She would pester him all night. If he wanted to get to his meal and that beer, he needed to get this over with. He called Prosperous into the living room to discuss her issues.

"Yes, Daddy," Prosperous said, looking like she was scared to come into the room.

"I expected for Dynamo to mess up and even Antenatal to mess up with their grades, but when you and Liberty bring those grades home, I want to know what the problem is. Out of all my children, you and Liberty are the smartest. Getting A's have always been an obsession with you. That's why I always held you two to that standard." He held up the progress report. "Can you explain to your mother and me why your grades seem to be dipping. Is there something going that you want to talk to us about?"

Prosperous stared at the floor, ashamed to look at her father. He wasn't yelling at her, but this was the closest thing to a scolding she'd ever received.

"The pressure that you all put on me to make perfect grades and to be perfect is getting hard. I want to make you all happy and to please you all, but it is hard. The teachers are starting to expect more of me and I am really starting to think

72

that they give me harder assignments than the rest of the class. I know that it is no excuse for my grades or my behavior, but can you please understand that it is affecting me?"

As Rhizome, listened to Prosperous, he understood where she was coming from and decided to give her a pass. Prosperous was shocked that her father did not spank her but was very thankful.

Time passed and Prosperous was able to pull her averages up. Nevertheless, she knew that she was not the highest ranked student in the school as she once was.

It was finally the last day that Prosperous would be in middle school and again the final day of rewards. What Prosperous hadn't realized is that she would be recognized for her perfect attendance and her hard work on her end of the year assignment. She wasn't aware that she would be recognized for anything because she knew that her grades had once dropped. She didn't know that she was the only person required to do the end of the year project and that the project was for a reason.

As the ceremony was beginning to start, Prosperous looked out in the crowd to make sure that the family was there to support her as usual. After not seeing them, she felt as if she had really disappointed them by not being number one this time. However, what she didn't realize was that the family was only running late.

As Prosperous got up to present her project, her family walked through the door. The sadness that she had on her face soon turned to a sigh of happiness. After completing her project her family stood and screamed in happiness for the success that Prosperous had.

When Prosperous and her family begin to leave out of the school, Rhizome grabbed her gently by the arm and forced her to lag back from her siblings so he could tell her something.

"I am proud of you," he said.

"Thanks, Daddy."

"You have greatness in you. I wouldn't say this in front of your sisters and brother, but I think you have the brightest future of them all. I want you to keep striving for greatness because I think you are going to make it."

"I appreciate you saying that. I want to travel the world and do exciting things. I want to see new things and meet new people. Whatever I do when I grow up, I'm going to always try to make you and mama proud of me."

Rhizome choked back a tear and hugged his daughter. She was his favorite, and at that moment, he didn't really care if anyone knew.

As the taxicab darted in and out of airport traffic and raced down the interstate, she wondered if her father would still consider her his favorite when she introduced her new husband to him. She hadn't told anyone, not even Liberty whom she was closest too, that she'd secretly gotten married.

The taxi pulled into the driveway. Prosperous and her new husband, Milton, got out of the car. Milton carried their bags up to the front door.

Prosperous took a deep breath and then pressed the doorbell. Moments later, Liberty answered the door.

"Prosperous!" she screamed. The two sisters hugged in the doorway. Liberty was holding her so tight that Prosperous thought she was going to suffocate.

"You gon' kill me, sis," Prosperous managed to say.

"I'm sorry," Liberty said, "I'm just so happy to see you." She looked over Prosperous' shoulder and saw the man holding her bags. "Thank you for carrying her bags. I'll take them from here."

"Oh, he's with me," Prosperous said. She looked at Milton and then back at Liberty. "This is Milton...my husband."

Liberty's eyes grew as wide as saucers. She reflexively covered her mouth. When she moved her hand from her mouth, she looked at Prosperous and said in a low tone, "But he's white."

Chapter 12

"Dynamo flipped through an old high school year book while his sisters were in the kitchen talking and preparing the meal. As he skimmed the black and white pictures of hundreds of pimple-faced teens, he spotted the picture of the girl that had broken his heart, Shanty. ' He closed the yearbook and stared aimlessly at the floor as he reminisced about what happened after he got caught leaving the letters in her locker.

One day Dynamo got a pass from the teacher to go to the bathroom during the class. When he left out of the classroom, he saw Shanty in that hallway. She was headed to the girl's bathroom.

"Hey, Dynamo," she said sheepishly.

Dynamo was too embarrassed to talk to so he pretended he didn't hear her.

"Dynamo, I know you hear me," Shanty shouted. "I'm trying to apologize to you."

"No need to apologize."

"But I want to explain something to you."

Dynamo stopped walking and turned around. Shanty grabbed his wrist and pulled him into a side hallway so they wouldn't be seen by a passing teacher.

"As hard as this may be for you to believe, going to the prom with you would be the most amazing thing that a girl could ever ask for." Shanty paused to wipe a few strands of dangling hair from in front of her eyes. "I do however, have one question, "Why did you leave all those notes in my locker? Why didn't you just tell me how you felt?"

"I believe that you are special, but I needed you to know and believe that you were special too." Dynamo said. "I left all of those notes in your locker because I believed that each one allowed you to see the real me."

Shanty had a pensive look on her face. After a few seconds of processing what he said and studying him, she said, "Be at my houses at 7:00 pm sharp and please don't be late."

It was prom night and Dynamo was picking up Shanty in a new Rose Royce, that he borrowed from his Uncle Patons Luxury Car Lot. What he didn't know was that Shanty would look so amazing that she would make him speechless when he saw her.

Upon arrival he parked the car in front of the sidewalk to her house and exited the car to ring her doorbell. Her mother opened the door and her father stood behind.

"Alright young man, I'm letting you take my daughter this prom, but I expect you to bring her home at a decent hour. And don't try any funny business with her. I always carry two loaded guns, just in case I need to use one."

"Yes, sir."

Dynamo was really shaken up but preceded to wait until Shanty came down the stairs.

Shanty ascended from the top of the stairs and down she came, in the cutest of Royal Blue dresses, with white pearl earrings, and Rhinestone trimmed designs throughout her dress. She looked like Cinderella going to the Prince's ball only more beautiful. She rendered Dynamo speechless.

As she made it to the end of the staircase, she said, "Hello, Dynamo. You look handsome."

"Thanks," Dynamo said. "Beautiful is not a word that can describe how great you look to me." Finally realizing that he was standing in front of her parents, he asked, "Can I place this corsage on your wrist."

"Yes, you may," said Shanty.

As her parents took pictures, while they were getting ready to leave out of the door, Shanty's father reminded Dynamo of the conversation being had before Shanty came down the stairs.

"Dynamo!" the tall well-built man called out. He patted his hip as if there was gun holster there and said, "Remember what I told you."

Dynamo went around to Shanty's door and opened. As she sat in the car, he closed the door behind her and proceeded to the driver side.

"Dynamo, this car is beautiful."

"Thanks. My uncle let me borrow it for tonight."

"After the prom, we've got to go riding around town. I want people to see me in this."

Dynamo heard her, but he couldn't reply. All he could think about was her father patting his hip as reminder of what he'd do if he didn't bring her home at a decent time.

Entering the doors of the prom everyone in the building got quiet. Shanty was the most popular girl in the school, but Dynamo was the most unpopular boy. To see the two of them at prom together made people speechless.

As they ignored everyone's awkward quietness, Dynamo asked, "Do you want something to drink?"

"Yes, please," she replied.

The theme for this year's prom was Cinderella and Shanty looked the part. As handsome as Dynamo was, he pulled off the title Prince Charming. Once the music started playing and people started having fun, everyone seemed to get over the surprise of seeing the two of them there. It was all about enjoying the night, and that is exactly what Dynamo and Shanty did. They laughed, they talked, and they danced.

The night was so young but it was also fun. The prom was coming to an end and Dynamo knew he needed to get Shanty home.

"Dynamo, why are we going straight back to my house?" asked Shanty.

"Because I promised your father that I would get you back home in a decent time," Dynamo replied, his hands clutching the steering wheel like it was life or death—because it was to him. He barely blinked as he stared out the window. "I don't want him to be mad."

"Why can't we just go to a room and well you know?" asked Shanty.

"I don't see you in that way Shanty. When the time comes for that we will do it, but right now, I have my entire senior year to worry about and I am trying hard not to disappoint my parents."

Shanty bottom jaw dropped. Her eyes grew wide. Frown lines raced across her forehead like bolts of lightning across the sky. She'd never had a boy refuse her advances.

"Dynamo, you are gay?" she asked. "A woman offers you the goods and you turn her down. You sure you don't want a man in your bed?"

Now Dynamo was the one with his mouth open and frown lines streaking across his head. She called him gay because he was trying to abide by her father's wishes.

As mad as he was, he desperately wanted to call her out of her name, but he knew that his parents wouldn't approve it. They didn't raise him in that manner.

He continued to stare out the front window and focus on the road ahead until he got back in front of Shanty's house. The entire way back, she cursed at him and called him out of his name, but he ignored her and just knew it was out of anger.

For the next few days, he tried to call her, thinking she might have calmed down from being rejected, but she never answered his phone calls. On the Monday after the prom, Dynamo went to school ready to swap prom stories with other classmates. He knew that the way he and Shanty looked that evening, and the fact that he had the fanciest car, was going to also make him more popular. But there was something Dynamo didn't know, and within five minutes of being in that school he was going to find out what it was.

Shanty was so angry of being rejected by him that when her girlfriends started swapping stories about the things that went down after the prom, she lied when they asked her.

"What did you and Dynamo do, Shanty?" asked one girl, chewing on gum and making it pop like she was starving.

"Nothing."

"What do you mean?"

"I mean just what I said," Shanty replied flippantly. "He took me straight home after the prom."

"But y'all had that fancy car and you looked so pretty. Y'all didn't go driving around?"

Another girl with purple streaks in her hair chimed in. "Well, if y'all didn't go driving around town to show off that pretty car, did y'all at least go to a hotel room?"

"No. I wanted to, but he didn't. I think he's gay."

That little statement was all it took to ruin Dynamo's high school experience. His reputation was already bad, and Shanty reckless remark only made things worse.

The rumor that he was gay spread like fire around the school. He wondered why so many people wanted to be his friend all of a sudden. It wasn't until it had gotten back to his father that he realized what had been said.

"Dynamo," his father said to him after he walked into the huge office, "please sit down."

"What's going on, Dad?"

"I have something I want to talk to you about."

"Is it my grades? I'm doing good in my class. I don't foresee any problems when it's time for me to walk across the stage."

"That's not it. I know your grades are good. I want you to explain what happened between you and Shanty after the prom. There is a rumor floating around that supposedly, you told her you were gay."

"That's not true!" Dynamo shouted and stood up.

"Calm down, calm down," Rhizome said. "I just want to hear your side of the story."

Dynamo spent the next ten minutes given a blow by blow account of what happened on prom night; from the moment he picked her up, the threat her father made, and even Shanty's desire to get a hotel room.

Rhizome listed intently. He didn't interrupt the boy once. When Dynamo finished talking, Rhizome scratched his beard for a moment and then put his elbows on his desk as he leaned in and said in a low voice, "Son, I love you either way, whether you are gay or not. I just want you to be happy and know that I am always here for you."

For the first time that Dynamo could remember, Rhizome showed compassion, he showed understanding, and even showed love. Dynamo didn't know what to make of this, he was confused as to why his father was so understanding of this.

Dynamo was in complete shock and for the first time in his life, he felt his father's love. He explained again to his father that he wasn't gay, but that he treated Shanty with respect as he had taught him. Even though he was impressed with his father's response, he didn't feel like he'd been heard.

"Dad, she wanted to go to a hotel room after Prom. I told her that I had promised her father I would get her home within a decent hour so that is what I did. She got mad because I refused to take her to a room and the first thing that came out of her mouth was that I was gay. I was not going to stop her from saying that because I know whom I am and I know how I have been raised. Do I care that everyone thinks I am gay? No! Why? Because none of them are doing anything for me."

Dynamo and his father continued to talk and after the bell sounded, he told Dynamo to go on to class.

Dynamo did as he was told, but when he got some time alone he wrote Shanty one last letter and stuck it into her wall locker"

"Dear Shanty, as judgmental as you are, I thank you for the lies that you have spreaded about me. Let me see if I can say this where you can understand. "I AM NOT GAY NOR HAVE I EVER BEEN GAY" However, due to your lies my relationship with my father has gotten better, my family seems to communicate more, and my sisters now realize just how a man is supposed to treat them. I thought that treating you like someone was something; as a woman I felt that you would appreciate it, but now I see that you like men treating you with much disrespect. I am not the one for you and I hope eventually you will see your worth and treat yourself with more respect."

P.S.
Please stop being judgmental of people when you have failed to actually get to know a person.

This was the letter that Shanty found inside of her locker. As she read over the letter and saw the things that Dynamo had said, she knew that she had made the biggest mistake of her life. However, she knew that she had lost Dynamo as well.

Summer was less than two days away and she knew that she needed but also wanted to apologize. However, that opportunity too had passed.

Summer had gone and passed and it was Dynamo's senior year. He was more focused on making sure that he did the right things and worked as hard as he could that year so that he could get the best scholarship available for college.

Dynamo wanted everything for his senior year to be as wonderful and special as Liberty's senior year was. He wanted his to be better so he took the necessary steps in order to make that a reality.

Dynamo entered school and was immediately greeted by his new girlfriend, Treasure. They had met over the summer while he was in camp. She had heard that he was gay at school, but wanted to know for herself if this was actually true.

Treasure was the type of young lady who didn't believe in listening to rumors. She preferred to ask questions and hear it from the person himself or herself. She was a woman who understands the art of communication and believed in it very much. She wanted her answers to come from the person whom they were about because only then she knew that it was true.

During the 4th of July celebration Dynamo and Treasure met in the square to see the fireworks and instantly something clicked within them. Treasure introduced herself and even told Dynamo that she went to school with him, he just never really noticed her.

Treasure was short, about 5'3" in height with a caramel complexion, however, she was a little on the heavier side. She was no cheerleader, but based on GPA's, she was the third smartest person within their class.

As they were talking to get to know each other, she told him that she had heard the rumors, but that was something that she didn't believe was true because she hadn't spoken with him

81

about it. She explained that she likes to hear what the individual who has rumors being spread around about them say before she takes the information and run with it.

Dynamo loved the vibe that he and Treasure had and knew that he needed to make her his girlfriend. Upon realizing this, he took it upon himself at that very moment to ask Treasure if she would like to go study with him. Treasure first told him no.

Treasure wanted Dynamo to be sure that he was over Shanty before she would go study with him so she asked that they take things slow and just get to know one another. As time passed over the summer, Dynamo and Treasure went out on a few dates and towards the end of the summer, Dynamo had gotten the answer he was looking for.

He called her one night and as Treasure would say, "The answer may not come when you want it to but when it does you will be happy."

As it turns out, Dynamo was exactly that. After the summer was over, he had an amazing girlfriend and one that he was destined to make just as happy as he was.

While in the hall, Dynamo kissed Treasure and explained that he wanted this year to be special for her just as it was going to be for him. He promised to give her time, patience, and commitment this year. Nevertheless, Treasure knew that whispers would flow within the hall about them because Shanty was still not quite over Dynamo. As much as she talked about how *gay* Dynamo was, she knew that her chance at happiness left the day she pushed Dynamo away.

About four months had passed since the beginning of school and Dynamo and Treasure had officially made everyone aware of their relationship within the school.

One morning in December, in the hall there was this big commotion and Dynamo could have sworn that he heard Treasure's voice. He figured if he was hearing her voice it had to be something big because you very rarely heard his girlfriend in the hall. He immediately jumped up out of the classroom and ran into the hallway to see exactly whom she was arguing with. His biggest question to her was why she was even arguing at all?

As he approached the situation, to his very surprise, it was Shanty and her and Treasure were going back and forth.

According to Shanty, Dynamo had been calling her for the past month because him and Treasure were having relationship issues. Naturally, Treasure was completely surprised by this confession. She thought that the discussions that she was having with Dynamo were strictly between the two of them; she didn't know Shanty was being included on the conversations.

"Is it true? Are you calling her?" Treasure shouted at Dynamo as he approached. "Why is Shanty approaching me about problems that we seem to be having and why wasn't I made aware that you were concerned about our relationship? Why are you even calling her in the first place?"

Without a word, Dynamo looked at Shanty with bucked eyes and a wide-open mouth, because he couldn't believe that the conversations that he was having with her about Treasure would be repeated back to her.

The thing that Treasure didn't know was that Dynamo and Shanty had discussed their issues and decided that they would become friends over the summer during the dating phase and getting to know stages of Dynamo and Treasure's relationship. What Dynamo didn't know was that even though Shanty was portraying herself to be his friend, she secretly was trying to find ways in which she could win Dynamo back over. Due to her and Dynamo talking on a regular basis, she started to see that she pushed away a really amazing guy and she was determined to try and get him back as soon as she could.

Treasure was so full of insecurities that she was pushing Dynamo to converse with Shanty to find out if their relationship broke up was because of him. Dynamo was only conversing with Shanty because he wanted to know from a female's perspective what could he as a man do in order to get his girlfriend to believe that he was only attracted to her and that his attention was only focused on her.

After realizing that Treasure had all of Dynamo's attention, Shanty didn't like that and so she plotted a way to ruin Dynamo and Treasure's relationship.

As Treasure stood there waiting on Dynamo to answer the question, she re-asked it aloud, "DYNAMO WHY IS SHANTY ASKING ME ABOUT MY RELATIONSHIP WITH YOU? IS THIS YOUR WAY OF BREAKING UP WITH ME?"

Without hesitation, Dynamo ran to Treasure's side and pulled her out of the hallway.

"Would you calm down. You are making a scene in this hallway," he said. "We will discuss this later on. I don't want everyone around this school to know what is going on in our relationship, and I will explain everything about Shanty to you as well."

As pissed as Treasure was, she was determined to not let anything mess up her relationship with Dynamo. She accepted his response and went back to class.

As Dynamo passed Shanty within the school, he had little respect for her.

"Dynamo, please let me explain," she said in front of a crowd of people.

"You don't have anything I want to hear. Lose my number!" Dynamo knew that it was time to cut all ties with Shanty once and for all. So, Dynamo texted Shanty and asked that she no longer contacted him. He was tired of the problems she brought and that he was better off without her in his life.

He even showed Treasure the text message that he sent to Shanty to prove that he was lying. It seemed to have worked because shortly thereafter, Treasure and Dynamo were seen in the hallway holding hands, smiling, and talking once again.

Weeks had passed and it was time for Christmas, to Treasure surprise, Dynamo invited her over to spend time with him and the family. Treasure was aware that Dynamo was the only boy of the four children; she just never imagined being asked over so soon.

"What if they don't like me?" Treasure asked.

"They're going to like you," Dynamo insisted.

Nevertheless, Dynamo could never able to prepare for what would happen when she met them. Dynamo did however, previously warned Treasure that his sisters and mother were no women to be messed with and to never lie when you meet them; they had a knack for catching you in all your lies.

Treasure wasn't the lying type so she was not going to lie anyway. Her biggest fear was whether they would think she was pretty enough for Dynamo. She'd seen all his sisters and they were all drop-dead gorgeous—especially, Antenatal.

"I have announcement everyone," Dynamo said at the dinner table one week before Christmas.

Rhizome dropped his fork. *Oh my God, he really is about to announce that he's gay.*

"I've decided to invite my girlfriend over for Christmas this year. As you all know, her name is Treasure. All I need from y'all is to be nice to her. She's nervous about coming here. PLEASE, PLEASE, PLEASE be on your BEST behavior. I really like Treasure and I think we could have a future together. I don't want y'all to scare her off."

Rhizome seemed to be happy with the news. Truth be told, he was just happy that Dynamo wasn't announcing that he was gay.

Malady wasn't so tickled. She threw her napkin on her plate and crossed her arms.

"Dynamo, you are too young to be talking about, or even know, what kind of woman you're going to have a life with. How are you to even know what you like when just last year you took Shanty to prom and now you are dating Treasure?"

Ignoring what his momma was saying Dynamo just smiled and stated again, "Because when you know, you just know."

Christmas arrived and the festivities were grand. The ground outside was covered with snow. Neighbors front lawns were decorated as if they were trying to compete with each. Christmas carols flooded the radio—everyone was happy.

For the first time in a long time, all the Watership children were in the same house and celebrating the holiday as a combined and unified family. The day seemed to be going very well. No disagreements amongst the women had occurred and Malady, Treasure, Prosperous, Antenatal, and Liberty were all in the kitchen getting the meal together.

When Treasure got up and excused herself to go to the bathroom, Dynamo took the opportunity to ask his family what they thought.

"Well, do y'all like her?"

"Seems like a nice girl," Rhizome said.

Dynamo looked at Malady. After all, it was her opinion that mattered most. "Well, Mama, what do you think of her?"

Malady desperately wanted to say something disparaging about Treasure. Maybe she didn't have good table manners. Maybe she was disrespectful and talked too much. Maybe she was too clingy to Dynamo in front of them. But none of those things were true. Treasure was perfectly mannered. She knew when to talk and when to shut up. She even brought small gifts for everyone. What was there not to like about her.

"I must admit," Malady said, "she is a sweet girl. I am very impressed with her."

Dynamo smiled with relief. As with all boys, impressing his mother was paramount.

"She's cute," Liberty said.

"I like her," Prosperous said.

"She's a'ight," Antenatal said. "Not somebody I would've chose for you, but if you like her…that's your choice."

"Why don't you like her?" Dynamo asked.

"She just acts kind of weird. You didn't see how she was looking while we were eating. She kept fidgeting and widening her eyes like she couldn't see good."

"She was just nervous," Liberty said. "Stop being so judgmental."

"I'm not being judgmental; I'm just giving my opinion."

While the kids argued in hushed tones, Malady noticed that Treasure had been gone an unusually long time.

"I'm going to go check on dessert," Malady said.

"I'll help, Mama," Liberty said.

"No, no, no," Malady insisted, "you sit down and talk to your siblings. I'll handle this."

Malady walked around the corner and made a beeline for the bathroom at the end of the hallway.

86

"Treasure," she said and knocked on the door lightly so that the rest of the family wouldn't hear.

"Treasure, are you okay?"

Treasure didn't respond so Malady turned the knob. What she saw shook her to her core. Treasure was on the bathroom floor unconscious. There was froth coming from her mouth.

Malady screamed so loud that everyone in the house came running. Rhizome pushed past his kids and knelt on the floor next to Treasure. He placed his fingers on her wrist to check for pulse and then on the side of the neck.

"Is she okay, Dad?" Dynamo asked.

Rhizome turned slowly and with a horrified look on his face replied, "I think she's dead, son."

As it turns out, Treasure had an enlarged heart. She was having problems breathing, which is why she'd been acting weird during dinner. Her death could have happened anywhere and anytime. Unfortunately, it happened on what was supposed to be the most joyous day of the year in their house.

The memories of that dreaded Christmas day haunted Dynamo. Seeing his first love be taken out of their house in a body bag. Seeing the despair on his family's face, and the faces of Treasure's parents. It was all too much for a boy his age to handle.

For months he refused to talk about it. Rhizome and Malady sent him to counseling, so that he could talk about his pain, but he refused to open up. Things got even worse for him when the rumor around school became that she Treasure died because of his mother's cooking.

When he graduated the only thing that he wanted to do was get as far away from their house as he could. So, with his diploma less than two weeks old, he walked straight into the army recruitment office and enlisted. He didn't care what career field they gave him, all he wanted was the fastest departure date they could offer.

Now that they were all assembled for Thanksgiving, the memories came back in waves. He just hoped he could remain sane long enough to finish his meal.

Chapter 13

Thanksgiving dinner was remarkable. Malady cooked the most elaborate meal that anyone could remember: a twenty-five-pound turkey, candied yam, stuffing, potato salad, and much, much, more.

Of course, all the great food couldn't sidetrack the obvious things that they needed to talk about.

Antenatal sat next to her son, RJ. Prosperous sat next to her white husband, Milton. Liberty sat next to Dynamo. And Rhizome and Malady sat at opposite ends of the long dining table.

For most of the dinner, everyone minded their manners and were very polite. Liberty spent much of the day staring at RJ. He was growing so fast. So handsome and full of life. He spent most of the day talking to Rhizome. Rhizome took him in the backyard and showed him the different pieces of lawn equipment that was used in the landscaping company. He even let the child sit atop of a huge riding lawnmower. The more Liberty stared, the more she thought about the child she almost had.

Her relationship with Bumper led to her getting pregnant. But she lost the baby. It wasn't due to any fault of her own. Some things just happen. Apparently, God wasn't ready for her to be a mother.

Still the experience was traumatizing. She'd lost the one thing in life that mattered the most to her. She didn't want Bumper to be around so she pushed him away the minute the doctors stated that the baby was gone.

Those were the most horrifying words that Liberty had ever heard in her life. She lost consciousness and couldn't breathe. She constantly blamed herself for the miscarriage that she had but not only that she hated herself even more because she couldn't believe that the only reason Bumper came back into her life was because of the baby. He tried on several occasions after the baby to show Liberty that he wanted to be there with her and for her, but she refused to allow him that opportunity.

Now, nearly ten years later, and she was still reeling from the pain. And looking at her beautiful nephew interact with his family—in particular, his grandfather—brought it all back to her.

"What's wrong with you?" Antenatal asked.

Liberty flinched. "What?"

"Why are you staring at my son? You've been sitting there staring at him. You're looking at him like you don't want him to be here."

"Oh, no, that's not it. I was just looking at how handsome he is," Liberty said.

"Stop lying!" Antenatal shouted. "You were staring at him because you don't think we belong here. I'm not married to his father and you look down on me for that. Go ahead and admit."

"Natal, what are you talking about?" Liberty asked, totally caught off guard by the outburst.

"Aww, Natal, calm down. We all love this child," Rhizome said. "This is my only grandson. He's going to be the person who takes over my business one day after I retire." He looked over at Dynamo. "I got to leave it to somebody since my own son thinks he's too good to work in landscaping."

"Dad, don't go there," Dynamo said. "I didn't join the army to get away from you or your business."

"No, you joined because you wanted to get far away from the secret that was going on around about you," Prosperous said.

"What secret?" Dynamo asked.

"Oh, you know…the secret that was going on around school that said you were…" she held out her hand and rocked it from side to side.

"That's a lie!" Dynamo said. "The reasons I joined the army ain't have nothing to do with that lie that Shanty started back in the day because I didn't want to date her."

"Well, you did move away and you never got married or even dated anyone that we've heard of," Prosperous said.

"Wait, wait, wait," Dynamo said and dropped his fork, "I know you ain't sitting here talking about me having a secret." He pointed at Milton who had his head down and was stuffing food into his mouth. "You're the one who went away to California and started living a secret life. Trying to convince everyone that you were being this little perfect Christian. When really, you were just out there dating white men. You even brough one home with you. Now *that's* a secret. Why don't you explain that?"

"I don't have to explain anything to anyone here. I am grown. I can do what I want to do."

Little RJ covered his ears when all the shouting started. He became so nervous and flustered that he wet his pants.

When he pushed his chair back from the table and ran out of the dining room crying, all the bickering stopped.

"See what y'all did!" Antenatal shouted. "Y'all upset him."

Antenatal stood up and was about to go and check on RJ, but Maladay—who'd been silent during all the arguing—spoke up.

"Sit down," Malady said.

"But Mama, I need to go check on my child."

Malady smacked the table with her open hand. "I said, sit down!" The room fell deathly silent. Malady pointed at Milton. "You go check on the boy while I speak to my kids. And don't come out until I call for you."

"Yes, ma'am," Milton said. "He wiped his mouth with a napkin and scurried out of the room like a scared roach.

Once Milton was gone, Malady placed her hands on the table and leaned forward.

"Every last one of you should be ashamed of yourselves. I called y'all together because its been years since we sat down as a family and had dinner. All I asked is that you try to be civil to each other for a few hours and you couldn't do that."

Malady scanned the table and decided to start from her right.

91

"Prosperous, your daddy and I have always gone light on you. You didn't grow up with the same strict rules that your siblings did. Mainly because we were both tired by the time you became a teenager. Your daddy was tired from running that business by himself and was getting sick.

"You went on and did some good things in your life and we never tried to hold you back. But now I see that maybe we weren't strict on you because you seem to have forgotten your home training. Just because you are grown doesn't give you the right to be irresponsible. There is no justification for you not telling your family that you were married and then just popping up here with Milton."

"But, Mama, I—"

"But nothing!" Malady cut her off. "It wasn't fair to us and it's not fair to poor Milton. You are his wife; you're supposed to protect your husband not put him in a position to feel uncomfortable." She rolled her eyes at her youngest child. "I guess you ain't grown enough to know that."

Malady looked over at Dynamo and shook her head, "Boy, your daddy is just hurt that you never really offered him a reason why you didn't want to run the company."

"Mama, it had nothing to do with not wanting to be here to take over the business," Dynamo said.

"I know that!" Malady snapped. "You left here because you couldn't stand being in the house where that girl, Treasure, died."

"That's the exact reason," Dynamo said.

"Then you should've been man enough to look your father in his eyes and tell him that. Instead, you run off and join the army without being truthful about your reasons. You might be a man, but the way you handled that was cowardly."

Malady looked at her husband and said, "And Rhizome, you need to understand that your dream may not necessarily be his dream. As parents, we are supposed to try to raise our kids and give them the tools to live a better life than the one we had. We are not supposed to try to force our dreams on them. Now, if he wants to run the company that's fine. But he has a desire to do something else with his life then you need to respect that."

"Malady, I worked my butt off trying to build something to pass on to my son. I was just disappointed that he didn't seem to want it. I felt like he was rejecting me."

"I know that's how you felt," Malady said. "That's why I brought up the real reason he left here today." She looked at Dynamo. "I was hoping he would get the guts to tell it to him yourself." She then looked back at Rhizome. "But I can't say that I blame him for not talking to you about it because you are unapproachable at times. As stubborn as a doggone mule. If you want people to talk to you, then you have to be easy to talk to."

Rhizome slouched in his chair like a scolded child and stared at his plate.

Malady looked at Antenatal. "Girl, I don't know what's wrong with you. You spend so much time playing the victim that you can't see your own flaws. All Liberty does is talk about how beautiful RJ is and how much she wishes she had a son like him. But you wouldn't know that because you stay away from us. You're so disappointed in yourself that you project that energy onto everyone else."

Malady started coughing and paused to drink her water.

"You know what your problem is, Natal, you've been so busy trying to compare yourself to Liberty and watching what she is doing that you haven't focused on getting your own life together." She pointed in the direction of the bedroom where RJ and Milton were. "It ain't your fault, that child's fault, or anyone at this table's fault, that Risque chose to abandon you and that child." She then wagged her finger at Antenatal. "But it is your fault that you don't bring him around us more often just because you are ashamed of yourself."

Malady started coughing again.

"Mama, are you okay?" Liberty asked and tried to grab her arm.

Malady swatted her arm away. "I'm fine, I'm fine," she said and sipped some water. "I ain't finished because I got something to tell you too, Liberty. Your siblings left the house and went out into the world and tried to find a life. Because of what you went through, you're too scared to leave.

"You are the oldest child. You're supposed to set an example for the rest of 'em. If Natal doesn't reach out to you, then doggone it, you pick up the phone and reach out to her. The reason she thinks you don't want RJ around and you're looking down on her is because you don't make enough of an effort to show her that you love her and her child."

Malady started coughing harder than she ever had. She coughed so hard that she had to cover her mouth with a napkin. Everyone stood up and tried to tend to her.

"Mama, are you okay?" Dynamo asked. "You are coughing like you are sick or something."

"I'm fine," Malady said.

Dynamo pointed at the napkin she had over her mouth. There was a big blood stain on it.

"Mama, you're coughing up blood," Prosperous said. "Something is wrong with you. We've got to get you to the hospital."

Malady waved them all away and pointed at their chairs. "Sit down. Please y'all, sit down."

"Mama, earlier you said something about being sick," Antenatal said, her voice trembling. "What's really going on with you?"

Malady wiped the blood from around her lips and glanced at Liberty. Liberty, whose eyes were filled with tears, nodded as if to tell her mother to confess.

"Tell 'em, Mama."

"Tell us what?" Dynamo said. "He looked at Rhizome. "Dad was is she talking about?"

Rhizome bit his lip and shook his head. Malady had already told him a week earlier that the cancer had spread and she didn't have much time left to live.

When she told him the diagnosis, he just sat quietly and stared while holding her hand. When she fell asleep, he went into the garage, grabbed a bottle of Gin that he kept hidden in a corner, and sipped it while sitting on his riding lawnmower. It was the best way he knew how to deaden the pain of knowing the love of his life would be leaving him soon.

Rhizome looked at his son and said, "It's your mothers call…she should be the person telling y'all."

Every person at the table looked at Malady at the same time. She took a deep breath and then exhaled. She extended her left hand and grabbed Liberty's hand and her right hand to grab hold of Prosperous.

"A few years ago, I was diagnosed with breast cancer. I didn't tell y'all because you were all out living your lives and I didn't want to be a burden. I didn't even tell your father because I didn't want him to worry. The only person who knew was Liberty and I only told her because I needed someone to drive me back and forth to the doctor's office when I became too sick to drive myself."

Antenatal looked at Liberty. Her eyes flickered with fire.

"Don't even think about saying anything to your sister, Natal. I made Liberty swear she wouldn't say anything. It's my illness so I get to tell my story when I'm good and ready." Malady sipped her water and then continued.

"After my most recent doctors' appointment last month, I got the news that my cancer has spread and I don't have much time left to live. Liberty was with me the day I got the news."

Liberty lowered her head and started crying. Antenatal watched her sister for a few seconds and then rubbed her back consolingly.

"That's why I had her call each of you and tell you I wanted you to come home for Thanksgiving," Malady said. "I told her to make the call and do not take, no, for an answer. And I forbade her from telling you all why it was important that y'all come."

Malady looked at each of her family members.

"Life is short," she said. "You all have different personalities and you've taken your own paths. I never stopped any of you. I may not have always agreed with your choices, but I never tried to stop you from charting your own course. All I did was try to love each of you in a way that fit your personalities." She released Prosperous' hand and pointed her wrinkle finger at each of them; slowly letting in glide in the space in front of her from right to left until she'd come full circle and stopped on Liberty. "After I'm gone, I need you all to promise that you are going to love each other unconditionally."

They all sobbed and nodded in agreement. Malady watched them all closely and then craned her neck and called out, "Milton!"

The bedroom door opened. "Yes ma'am."

"You can come out now baby and bring RJ with you."

Milton and RJ came out of the room.

"Umm, Ms. Watership," Milton said sounding nervous, "I hope you don't mind, but I realized we were in Dynamo's old bedroom. I figured it was worth a shot to see if I could find some old shorts that RJ could slip into. I grabbed an old pair of basketball shorts with a drawstring that I could tighten so they wouldn't fall off."

Malady looked at Prosperous and said, "He's smart." She then looked at Milton and winked. "Come here baby," she said and held out her arms to receive RJ. The boy hugged her and sat and stood next to her with his arm draped around her neck.

"I know they might have scared you earlier with all of that hooting and hollering, but they didn't mean to." She paused to look at everyone and then grabbed RJ's chin. "Look around this room child, this here is your family. And ain't nothin' more important in this world than family. We don't always get along, but when it's all said and done, family is all you got. Do you understand me?"

"Yes, ma'am," RJ said.

She pointed at Dynamo. "I expect you to take leave or do whatever it is Uncle Sam will let you do to come home and be a positive role model in your nephew's life. Do you understand me?"

Malady looked at Antenatal. "And you don't give your brother a hard time about it. I don't care how good of a mother you are; a woman can't teach a boy how to grow up and be a man—I don't care how hard she tries. He needs his uncle. Are we clear?"

"Yes ma'am," Antenatal whispered.

Malady looked at Milton. Before she could say a word, he spoke up.

"Yes ma'am. As his uncle, I promise I'm going to make myself available to him whenever he needs me. I promise you that Mrs. Watership."

Malady smiled and said in a calming voice, "Just call me, Mama."

Milton smiled. "Yes…Mama."

Malady looked at Rhizome. "If he wants to run the company one day, teach him. If he doesn't want to, you leave him alone about it. If you get tired of running it then sell the company and use the money to invest in whatever dream he has."

"Yes, baby," Rhizome said.

Malady looked at her three girls and said, "And as for the three of you…I expect y'all to treat each other like sisters and not rivals. I don't know what y'all gotta do to strengthen your bond, but I expect you to figure it out. Is that understood?"

"Yes, ma'am," they all said in unison.

"Now, I'm still hungry and I'm ready to finish my dinner." Malady held out her hands. "Y'all come give me a hug so we can get back to eating Thanksgiving dinner like we got some sense."

They all ascended on Malady like a bunch of vultures tearing away at roadkill. Her arms weren't wide enough to embrace them all at the same time, but her heart was wide enough to take them on with no problem.

Chapter 14

Malady died in her sleep six days later, on New Year's Eve. Rhizome said she had a smile on her face and was holding an old picture of the two of them when they were first married. She was fifty years old.

The funeral was packed with family, friends, church members, and a host of people whom she'd never met, but they knew of her and wanted to pay their respects.

The entire family sat in the first two pews of the church. The girls all sobbed uncontrollably, but the men were strong. Rhizome, Dynamo, Milton, and even little RJ, comforted the women and held their heads high with dignity just like Malady would have expected them too.

At the repast, which was held at the house, the family welcomed a crowd of people who still wanted to offer their condolences. While the sisters carried themselves with the grace that their mother tried to instill in them, Rhizome and Dynamo stood off to the side and watched.

"You sent her home in style, Dad," Dynamo whispered.

"Thanks, son. Your mother was a queen and deserved to be buried like one."

"No argument here," Dynamo said. "By the way, things have been so hectic and emotional that I forgot to tell you something."

"What's that?"

"Well, I've been doing a lot of thinking about what went down on Thanksgiving Day and all of the things that Mama said. She was absolutely right—I did stay away because of what happened here with Treasure. That incident is really what made me join the army. Now that I've served my country for a few years, I've decided to get out."

Rhizome looked surprised. "Are you serious? I just assumed you'd make it a career."

"I thought about it, but the more I've been thinking, I realize that I'm not as happy being in as I once was. I'm tired of having my life controlled by military rules. It's time for a change."

"I can understand that," Rhizome said and sipped his coffee. "Have you thought about what you're going to do once you get out. How's the job market in Georgia?"

"I don't know how the job market is in Georgia because to be honest with you, Dad, I have no desire to stay there."

"Where are you moving too?"

"I was going to move back here to Texas. I was hoping I could move back in here for a while…if that's okay with you…and learn the family business from the ground up."

"Son, it's an emotional time. Maybe you should think about this a little harder and longer before you make any rash decisions."

Dynamo placed his hand on his father's shoulder. "I have thought about it, Dad. I've thought long and hard about it. I admire the fact that after you stopped teaching you had the courage to start your own business. After living that regimented lifestyle: being where to live, what to wear, and in some case, barked at by lesser men, I know that I need to be my own boss too. I wanna be like you. I wanna learn how to run the family business so that I can take over one day when you are ready to step down. Will you teach me?"

Rhizome tried to hold in his tears, but seeing all those people dressed in black and wandering his house, coupled with the announcement that his only son had just made in his ear, made the flood gates open. The man who never cried started sobbing uncontrollably.

Rhizome's body slumped to the point that his knees almost touched the floor. Dynamo caught his father and helped him back to his feet.

"I got you, Dad," Dynamo whispered.

The two men embraced and stood there crying on each other's shoulders. The embrace lasted for more than a minute.

While they hugged each other, Rhizome whispered into Dynamo's ear, "Thanks, son, you have no idea how much I needed to hear you say that to me."

Dynamo, who was now sobbing just as hard, said into his father's ear, "Dad, you have no idea of how long I've been wanting to say that to you. I just didn't know how."

The repast lasted for another few hours. Eventually, the well-wishers stopped coming and started filtering out of the house. The entire family pitched into to clean up the place and make it as pristine as Malady always kept it—there were few things she hated more than a dirty house.

By nightfall, the kids all started to leave. First Prosperous and Milton. Then Antenatal and RJ. Dynamo caught an Uber and headed straight to the airport so that he could get back to base on time. Liberty, who still lived at home, decided to take a ride with a young man she'd met the day after Thanksgiving named, Fanciable Floridalicious, Jr.

They met when she was on her way to the doctor and he accidentally bumped into her. That accident turned into daily phone conversations and a lunch date. Although they hadn't known each other for a full week before Malady died, Fanciable still sent flowers and attended the funeral.

When it was all over, Rhizome sat alone in his favorite chair. He grabbed a beer and stared at the TV with the volume turned down. Alone with nothing but his thoughts, he reflected on all the beautiful moments he shared with Malady: from the day they married to the birth of each of their kids. It had been a rollercoaster ride, but one he was so happy to have taken with her.

He sipped his ice-cold beer and spoke as if she was sitting across from him in her favorite chair.

"I want to thank you for getting our family back together before you left me. You always were the backbone of this family. We would be lost without you." He smiled and wiped a tear. "We sure went through a lot together baby. The road wasn't always smooth, but doggone it, we made it through. And for that my dear, I thank you."